PLAYING TO WIN

Billionaire Playboys
Book 5

TORY BAKER

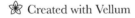 Created with Vellum

Prologue

DANICA

Seven Years Earlier

"IF YOU WALK OUT OF THAT DOOR, YOUNG LADY, don't come back, not ever!" Those are the last words I hear as the door softly closes behind me, taking everything I can in my small duffle bag and backpack, with only the money I earned from my job working as a cashier in the all-natural, uber-organic grocery store the past two years to my name. The man who just spewed those last words, he's full of hate and self-right-eousness in his narcissistic behavior. The kicker of it all, my own flesh and blood didn't do a damn thing to stop him. My mom stood right beside him as her husband chewed my ass out over the simplest of things. This time, it was

1

because I got home too late from work. My job is my saving grace, picking up as many hours as I can to stay out of the house, away from anything and everything Charles Masterson. His lecherous eyes and perverted words he uses when Mom isn't around are despicable. Earlier this week, he commented that my skirt should be shorter when his business associates are over for dinner. I didn't say a word and bit the inside of my cheek so hard I tasted blood. It's a miracle I made it through the dinner, excusing myself as fast as I could only to lock myself in my room, my desk door underneath the handle to keep myself as safe as possible. The time was coming for me to leave, or I'd be used in a way no woman should ever be if she doesn't want that life for herself.

When Charles started on his bullshit the minute I walked through the door, ignoring him was the only option. My bag was already packed in preparedness, though I'd hoped to at least get through my senior year of high school. I guess my luck ran out. It's better this way—for my dignity, my sanity, and my safety. With that thought, I throw my middle finger up, giving him and my mother the best salute there is, even if they can't see it through the upper Manhattan super-elite-of-the-elite apartment. How my mother ever fell for someone as disgusting as Charles Masterson I have no idea. I mean, sure, living in poverty isn't fun, but I'd rather be poor and hungry than be taken against my will. I shake my head in disgust as I head to the women's shelter to see if there's a room I can use until I figure out my next move.

"Danica, wait! Dani!" I hear my name off in the distance. My eyes move from one corner to the other, trying to figure out where my mother's voice is coming from. She's the epitome of style, grace, and demure, a Stepford wife through and through these days. Another side effect from Charles Masterson. And if he saw her running, he'd have an absolute coronary.

"Mom, go back inside. I'll be fine." She can't choose between me and her husband. Really, she shouldn't either. I'm eighteen now, responsible for myself. There are two more months between me and my next goal. Accomplishing going to school while being homeless might put a damper in things, but where there's a will, there's a way.

"Take this, Danica, and get the hell out of this place." My mom's usually perfectly styled hair is messed up from the wind plus running. How she managed to run in heels without falling flat on her face obviously took some practice. That isn't what has me staggering back, though. Nope, that would be the now unconcealed marks along her neck. I'm shaken to my core, shocked beyond disbelief when I shouldn't be. Charles Masterson is a monster, hiding beneath five-thousand-dollar suits, millions of dollars, and a smug smile.

"Come with me. Don't go back, please." We may not have the best relationship since Charles entered the picture, but that doesn't mean I want any ill will brought to her. She is my mother after all. Which is why a lump is forming in the back of my throat, causing me to lose what little oxygen I had and making it hard to finish my next sentence.

"I can't, but you can get out of here. Take this. There's money, your birth certificate, and a few other things. Go be free, sweetheart. I love you." I wrap my arms around her body, hugging her tightly like I used to before bed each night and early in the morning when she was sending me off to school.

"I love you, too, Mom." Her body is rigid within our embrace, a small whimper leaves her lips, and I know she's staying back for reasons I'm unprepared to think about. I soak in the last time I'll probably have her like this. It sucks. The whole situation does. How she got wrapped up in Charles Masterson I have no idea, and her choosing to stay isn't helping matters.

"I love you, Danica, never forget." She pulls away abruptly, spins on her heels, and runs like the fire from hell is after her. That's when I make a promise to myself: never ever get involved with a man who has charm and billions. Little did I know that seven years later, I'd be doing exactly that.

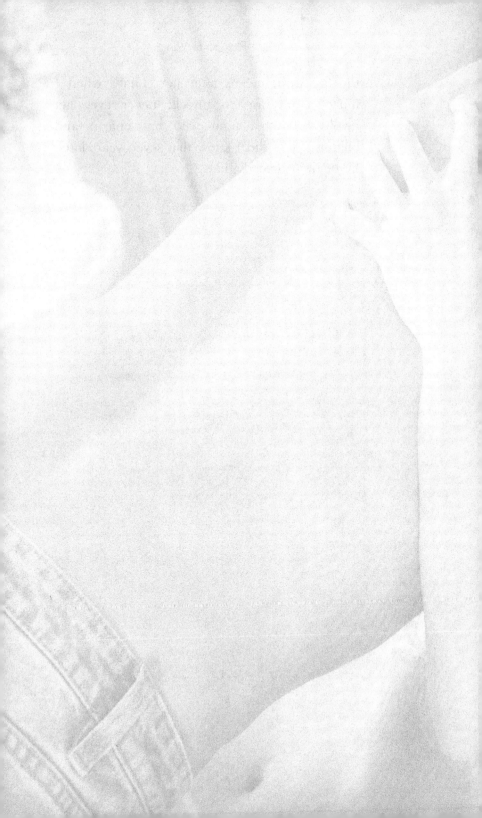

ONE

Theo
_____

Present Day

"WE'LL DISCUSS IT AT TOMORROW'S MEETING.
I've just walked in on a woman on her and
hands knees." Parker is on the other end of the
line. An exasperated breath leaves him. I don't
elaborate. I hang up the phone, pissing him off
further, meaning I'll get a ration of hell
tomorrow at our once-a-month meeting. A
meeting that could be an email, but it's the one
time a month we all get together—Parker, Ezra,
Boston via a Zoom call, and Sylvester in case
there's some new investment we all want to take
part in.

I pocket my phone, wondering why the hell the
woman in front of me is scrubbing the floor in

the kitchen. Her strawberry-blonde hair is in a ponytail and she has an hourglass figure, her back arched and ass tipped up in a way that would have any man dropping to his knees. My hands flex before tightening in a fist, imagining what it would be like to grip her tiny waist and pull her back onto my cock. I've yet to see the front of the woman who has my cock going from a flaccid state to a semi in a matter of seconds. It doesn't help matters when she sways her hips in the tight denim shorts barely covering her ass, right to left then left to right. Toned and lean thighs give way to legs that remind me of a dancer, and the white canvas shoes finish the bottom half. My eyes rove upwards. Her lower back is showing, the white men's wife beater she seems to be wearing doing little to hide the tattoo on her lower back or the bra she wears beneath. It's then I notice she's got earbuds in both ears as one hand scrubs the marble floor while the other holds her up.

The last time the cleaning company sent someone over, they made themselves at home, eating my food, watching TV, and even using my computer. Today, they scheduled a new employee. I wasn't willing to take any chance and have a repeat performance. In all actuality, I should have fired Clean and Gleam, probably would have, too, if they didn't take care of Four Brothers, my place, and everyone else in our friend group, plus they made it right. It saved me the headache of having to find another company, and damn it's making it hard to be upset with them with my current view. I walk around, watching the way her tits bounce with every movement she makes, seeing her lips say something, but I can't decipher it. Once I'm in front of the woman, she still doesn't look up or feel my presence. A protective feeling I've never felt before hits me in my gut. How is it she can be in a stranger's home and so unaware of her surroundings? I drop down to my haunches, hand reaching out to take one of her earbuds out, and that's when she lets out a glass-shattering scream.

"Oh, my fucking God! What is wrong with you!" It's not a question. She's shouting the whole damn place down. The lack of furniture and shit most people collect doesn't help with her echo. That along with the floor-to-ceiling windows, yeah, I'm sure the neighbors below me could hear the banshee. I'd have answered her scream if it weren't for the wet rag that hits me square in the chest, soaking my shirt while dirtying me, I'm sure.

"Me? You're in my home." The front is even better than the back. I didn't think that was possible. She's sprawled out, ass to the floor, feet planted on the ground, legs spread and hands behind her back. A look of confusion is written on her face. She's got light green eyes, full plush lips, and a face devoid of any type of makeup, thank fucking God. All natural, just like the rest of her body, as her tits move with each deep inhale and exhale she takes. I've watched each and every one of the men who are like family fall, hard and fast. I never thought it'd happen to me, yet here's this tiny woman, much smaller than my six-foot-two frame, and I'm having thoughts about keeping her.

"You still could have tapped me on the shoulder or something." Oh, she's big fucking mad. Good. That makes the two of us. I have no idea who else she cleans houses for with Clean and Gleam, but she won't be doing those ever again.

"Sorry about that." My apology is insincere.

"I told Mallory I didn't want to work at this place," she mumbles low, probably thinking I can't hear her. I stand up from my perch and take a hesitant step toward the woman, walking around the wet area she was working on. As much as I'm sure she'd like me to fall flat on my face, making an ass out of myself is not in the cards today.

"And what's wrong with this place?" I hold my hand out, offering to help her up. The little firecracker waves my hand away. I'm relentless in staying where I am. So, when she's off her feet, the fairy of a woman, it's just as I assumed— she's fucking tiny in height and stature. I'm head and shoulders taller than her, and I'd bet anything I could carry her with little to no effort.

"It's not the place. It's the people." I arch my eyebrow, waiting for her to elaborate.

"I'm almost done for the day, then I'll be out of your way." It's clear as day I won't be getting a response, choosing to step aside as she takes a step forward, shoulders squared, ready to attack. Yep, I'll be making a call to Clean and Gleam. I'll do whatever it takes to make sure she keeps working in my penthouse and no one else's.

TWO

Danica

"DON'T GO THERE," I MUTTER UNDER MY breath as I resume my task of scrubbing the floor. The man whose name is Theo Goldman, co-owner of Four Brothers, a billion-dollar company, is a man I want nothing to do with. A man in a business suit that costs three times more than my monthly rent. Hell, his shoes would cover at least one month. It brings up a past I'd like to keep buried, a time when money was the key to everything, except it wasn't. I shake my head. No way, not today, Satan. It's bad enough the penthouse owner already caught me unaware. A practice I try to never allow to happen. I'm usually on my A-game, careful, watchful, and alert. Theo Goldman wasn't due home while I was cleaning today. This job also should have been easy, but it wasn't. The penthouse wasn't disgustingly filthy by any means, but when you really looked at the kitchen counters, refrigerator, behind the toilets, and the floor, well, that was an entirely different story—dust, dirt, grime, and crumbs were definitely there. I got lost in my task with both earbuds back in, noise cancellation turned off, so I could hear what was going on around me while still listening to the sultry song, a guitar riff tearing it up, the male singer giving what I'm sure is the lead guitarist his moment. Still, I didn't hear him, which sucks because I was too in the moment.

My eyes catch on a pair of black shoes leaving the area, allowing me to breathe a sigh of relief. Now, if I could tell my dumb body that he's nothing, he's nobody, just another male body. Except I can't get over the way I reacted to him. Seven years I've gone against the grain, so to speak, using a man for one night and one night only. I'd sneak out of their bed the next morning, never to see them again. I also made sure they never wore a suit. We'd meet at a place a wealthy person would never step foot inside of, and no numbers are ever exchanged. I made the rules, stuck with them, and never put myself in a situation where I'd be dependent on a man. Maybe it's been too long sing I've been on or under a man because the way Theo made me feel, it's different. It didn't matter that his presence was twice that of mine; he didn't come off as someone who would use their body against someone unwillingly. Theo Goldman came off as mischievous, alluring, and, I'm not ashamed to admit, ridiculously handsome.

My body is doing traitorous things to me, like my core clenching and nipples tightening. The fire inside me plus being annoyed with myself only makes me clean the floors harder and faster in an effort to get out of here as soon as possible. I pretend I'm scrubbing him from my memory bank—his ungodly tall figure, light chocolate brown hair, whisky-colored eyes, bronze skin, and clean-shaven face. Maybe it was the way he discarded his suit jacket, leaving him in a long-sleeved black button-down shirt, the cuffs of his sleeves folded back, showing off deep veins running along the top until they rotate toward the inside and reach his wrist. Yep, for someone who wants to cut off a certain male species, I'm sure doing a bang-up job of forgetting about Theo Goldman. I move to another spot after working on the same area for the past too many minutes, cursing myself internally while having thoughts about Theo as if he'd give me the time of day, or that I'd give him the time of day. This is my last task for the day. I already cleaned the rest of the penthouse. Another thought attacks me after meeting the owner—his bedroom. The floor-to-ceiling windows are carried out through the entirety of his house, including his bedroom, where I changed the dark black bedding. His rich black currant with a mix of tobacco almost overwhelmed me. The scent matches its owner, completely and overwhelmingly.

I finish up the last portion of flooring and make a mental note to tell Mallory to pay me more for this job. Clean and Gleam doesn't skimp when it comes to paychecks. The fact that I'm in my fourth year of college as a twenty-five-year-old says a lot. I worked two jobs to afford my small postage stamp apartment, saving up as much as I can in order to pay cash for school. I'd need another payment like I need a hole in my head. So, while yes, I'm older than most students in my class, at least one day, years later than I'd initially wanted, I'll come out on top while being debt free. College isn't cheap, especially for what I'm going for—an ultrasound technician. The pre-requisites were holding me back, and night school after working ten-hour days cleaning made it even harder.

"Finally." I throw the rag into the mop bucket and take my earbuds out, pocketing them in my jean shorts. It wasn't smart of me to wear them, but when Mallory called saying it was a 9-1-1, that I needed to fit this last job in and that the owner would be out, I wore my usual when I'm cleaning. Except I'm always by myself. Today was an anomaly. It's the tank top that has me re-thinking things. New York is experiencing a heat wave, so sweating any more than necessary seemed stupid. My hands go to my lower back as I arch it in a stretch. A heating pad will most assuredly be my best friend tonight, along with a Coke. I'll need the caffeine to finish my homework before tomorrow night's class, and I know Mallory will have my schedule packed tomorrow, too.

I stand up, grab my bucket, and walk toward the half bathroom to dump the nasty water, clean the toilet, then call it a day. Anything else will have to wait until next week. I've been here for too long as it is and way past my quitting time, which means I'll miss the train I need to take. Walking home is going to be a bitch but nothing I haven't handled before. Except today, my back hurts and my knees are snap, cracking and popping from all the work I've done, plus my period is due, which makes me one cranking bitch. That's probably why I'm not paying a lick of attention at where I'm going with two hands holding the bucket, arms weak. And smack hard into a solid mass of muscle.

"Shit, shit, shit." The cuss words are out before I can stop them. Mallory is going to kill me if Theo reports every single incident that happened today, and I'll be out of a job. Jesus, it's like today is trying to kill me the fuck off.

THREE

Theo

"WHOA, ARE YOU OKAY?" MY HANDS GO TO HER shoulders, holding her steady so she doesn't slip in the water that's currently soaking both of our lower bodies. I was walking toward the kitchen, needing something to eat after working at the office longer than I'd have liked. Four Brothers is looking at acquiring another business, this time a bank. We've never taken over something this substantial, meaning there's a shit ton that can and I'm sure will go wrong. So, I spent most of the day pouring over the numbers as well as working with our specialist in fraud to see where the money went and why a bank is on the verge of bankruptcy before we take the final step. A lot of things aren't adding up. There's no reason a bank should be hemorrhaging money. Especially one of this caliber. Evertrust has been around for nearly seven decades. The president right now is the one who came to Four Brothers asking for a merger—our name, our money—all while he remains owner at fifty percent.

"I'm so sorry," says the woman whose mouth seems to run away from her whenever I'm near. Danica currently has her forearm over her mouth, probably to cover up the litany of curse words she just let lose. While in my home office, I went through my personal email, finding Clean and Gleam's in order to finally put a name to the face in my house.

"It's not a big deal. Stay where you are. I'll go grab a few towels," I offer. She's already shaking her head no.

"No, I will. I'm in sneakers. Your shoes are no match for wet marble flooring, and, well, this is my job." She takes off, her body leaving my hands faster than I would have liked. My cock jerks beneath my pants as I watch her cute little ass bounce with every step she takes in those sinful jean shorts. I should be going after her, not standing here like I've got my dick in the dirt, hunkered down in a desert waiting for a sniper to pick me off. I'm about to follow her when she's rushing out of the room, whispering to what I assume she thinks is herself, except my ears are ridiculous, and I can hear more than I care to.

"I'm going to lose my job and a ride home if I don't hurry this along." A few towels are bundled in her arms, and she's got a look of sheer determination on her face. The weight of the world may be on her shoulders, but Danica isn't crumbling like so many others would. I'm stunned stone-cold silent when she drops to her knees. Jesus fucking Christ, my restraint is about to come undone. She doesn't use the wall or my hand to steady herself as she lowers her body to the floor, and damn if my cock doesn't harden further. A thought hits me. I gave my friends, who are so much like brothers, a ration of hell. Each of them is tied in fucking knots over their women. Women who are now like sisters to me by way of marriage. A couple of them even have kids. On the rare occurrences we all get together, I'd tell them there was no damn way I'd ever be strapped to a woman. Yet one tiny little woman who's on her knees in front of me has me rethinking every single thought I've ever had.

"That's enough, Danica." The strawberry-blonde crown of her head tips back. Her lips are pursed, eyes narrowed, and all I can do is smirk.

"How do you know my name? I didn't give it to you." There's a note of worry in her tone as she drops the towels beside the mop bucket and stands up, staggering back a step or two. A bad feeling takes hold of me. There's more to Danica than her working for Clean and Gleam.

"Mallory sent me an email with your name in it." I don't elaborate that her boss, whom I've had under my employment for many years, has always had this protocol. Now not only is Danica on high alert, so fucking am I. A range of expressions crosses her face before worry and shock transform into a look of indifference. It's her hands balled into tight fists at her sides that gives her away. "Leave it. I'll take care of the rest. You've done more than anyone else has, and it's me who's causing the extra mess."

"Crap, I should have thought about that. I usually work in the corporate offices, where there's no one except a few other employees." She bends down to grab the towels and mop bucket.

"Danica, hand it over. I'll take care of that. You mentioned something about missing a ride?" I question, stepping closer to her in order to take the items from her hands since she's standing still, unmoving, with her head cocked to the side.

"No. It's too late now. I've missed the train, and the next one won't arrive for another couple of hours. I'd have had to leave ten minutes ago. I'll finish this up and then order a car." She checks the watch on her left wrist, one of those that isn't a smartwatch like most everyone wears these days but a run-of-the-mill basic one that looks well worn, going hand in hand with the defeat currently rolling through her body.

"I'll take you home. It's my fault you're running late." I'm not giving her an option. There's no way I want her in the back of a car where who knows who is behind the wheel.

"Mr. Goldman, I appreciate the gesture, but I'll be okay. I always am," she mumbles as I take the bucket from her hands. The grip she has on the towels says enough. Clearly, Danica will handle them.

"Theo. Call me Theo." One more step, and I'd be close enough to touch her. I also see she's reluctant in that aspect, which is why I stay where I am but continue the conversation. "Non-negotiable. I'm driving you home. You want someone to vouch for me, I'll give you my brothers' numbers. Call them. Mallory will do the same." Danica's nod is hesitant. Either she really needs to get home, or the ride will set her back financially. Regardless, it's a win in my book.

FOUR

Danica
_____

I'M GOING WITH MY GUT, THAT'S THE ONLY
logical explanation I can give as to why I
relented so easily when Theo offered to give me
a ride to my apartment. The thought of waiting
for a ride, bus, or train had me ready to bite my
nails down to the quick. At this rate, I'm without
a doubt going to be late for class tonight, for the
first time ever during my final year in college, so
close but still so far away. Sure, he told me I
could call one of his friends from the well-
known Four Brothers Incorporated, or call
Mallory, but there was no way I'd call my boss.
As cool and laid back as she is, this wouldn't be
okay with her, and asking his friends for what? A
background check? As if that would help. I only
hope my instinct doesn't get me killed.

"I need an address if I'm going to get you home
anytime soon," Theo says after pulling out of

his parking spot in a vehicle I'm all too knowledgeable about how many zeros are in its price. Much like his penthouse, the black-on-black luxury sports car goes with his personality.

"Amelia and West 304th Street." I don't give him the exact location of my apartment. I do have some sense of self-preservation.

"Alright," Theo responds while he's looking both ways before pulling out of the parking garage. I'm doing everything in my power not to look at him, but it's kind of hard when nothing else seems to be holding your attention. His hand is on the gear shifter in the center console, and his firm thighs move seamlessly as he goes from first gear and drops into second. That's when my gaze zeroes in on his muscular forearm, watching each flex and pull. It's porn for women of all kinds, there's no two ways about it.

"So, tell me about yourself, Danica." Our eyes collide. The tilt of his lips tells me I've been caught staring. I pull myself away from his warm eyes. The back of my head meets the headrest, and I close my eyes, gathering my thoughts and composure. There's something about Theo. He makes me want to do the unthinkable—trust a man who's worth billions.

"Hmm, well, I work at Clean and Gleam full-time, have for years now." A shiver runs down my spine thinking about how I thought my eighteen-year-old self could bounce right back with the wad of cash my mother gave me. It was a hope and a prayer. It wasn't until after staying at the women's shelter for nearly a week that Mallory hired me on. I worked a few hours a day while completing my high school career in the form of a GED at the women's shelter. As much shit as she gives me, I give it right back, and even when I joke that she'd fire me, I know she wouldn't. It's also why I usually have the choice of where I work. "I also work at a bar a few Saturdays a month when there's a concert and they need a second set of hands. After working for Mallory, I head to night classes at the local college." The money from the bar is pocketed away, a fallback in case there's ever a time dear old stepdad decides to come looking and I need to get the fuck out of town. It's been seven years. There's no reason for him to try and find me. Unless something happens to my mom.

"Do you ever sleep? It's kind of hard to do it all with the schedule you're handling." I want to roll my eyes. Oh, I'm handling life alright. That being said, men should never underestimate the power of a woman who is determined.

"Every night for at least six to seven hours. Sundays are my one day off a week." I shrug my shoulders. Not that Theo can see the gesture; he's maneuvering the car with careful precision, weaving in and out of traffic. I have no doubt he could drive the streets of New York in his sleep,

27

unlike myself. I have a license. I use Clean and Gleam as my address for the majority of my bills and packages I order as well. Did I mention Mallory is a freaking saint?

"You can stop here," I tell Theo when he's at a stop light a block from the front of my building.

"Not fucking likely. I'll park and walk you up." This time, I really can't contain myself. My eyes roll in a fluttering of lashes, and I cross my arms over my chest, causing me to look down my body. Theo is in his several-thousand-dollar suit, while I'm in a white tank I found in the clearance bin, jean shorts from jeans that had more holes than I could repair, and shoes that are beyond scuffed up. We're complete opposites in every way imaginable, yet Theo seems not to care.

"Theo, I, um… Yeah, well, this isn't the best area, and while I appreciate you walking me up to my apartment, it's probably not a good idea." My words fall on deaf ears. "Don't tell me I didn't warn you." He does the impossible and finds a parking spot along the curb at this time of day. Never have I seen one around at this hour. Luck must run through his veins.

"It'll be fine. Now you want to tell me which building is yours?"

"That one, a few stoops up the street." I nod toward the brick building. He grumbles something, but I don't catch it. He's busy opening his door, unfolding from his seat, then closing the door, and then it's me scrambling from my seat. I grab my small bag by my feet, hand going to the door to open it, when Theo appears.

"Ready?" His hand is out, giving me no other option except to take it, and when I do, I'm not prepared for the way he makes me feel. I am well and truly fucked.

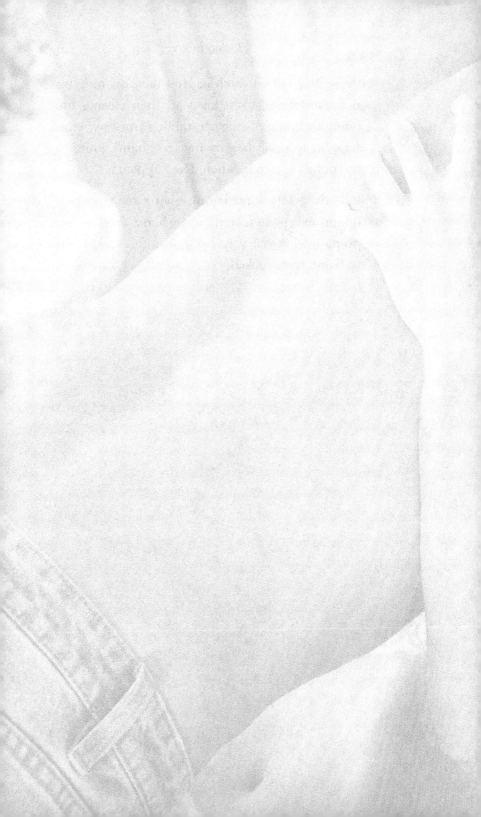

FIVE

Theo

I DON'T LET HER HAND GO, NOT WHEN SHE'S OUT of the car, standing beside me, not when we're walking up toward her apartment. Danica tried to take her hand away from mine, but I wasn't having it, pulling her closer to my body in order to avoid others on the sidewalk and keeping her there. The way she made it seem when I parked my car was that the neighborhood isn't all that great, and while I can understand where she's coming from, I'm pretty sure in the ten minutes it takes me to walk her, I won't walk back out to someone having hot wired my car. In fact, I'd like to see them fucking try. The car is equipped with more shit than even I was aware, auto locking itself down if someone tries to tamper with the handle. The most that could happen is I'd come out with the car on jacks with no tires.

"This is me," Danica says once we stop in front of her building. I look at her. She tightens her hold on the backpack strap, gripping it as if it were a life vest and she's stranded out at sea.

"Lead the way. I'll walk you to your door, and then you can get rid of me." I wink, teasing her. Never in my life have I had to work to get a woman to at least pretend to like me. God, if my fucking brothers could see me now, they'd be having the last laugh.

"Theo, you've done more than enough. I'm sure you have better things to do with your evening than walk up three flights of stairs to watch me walk inside." My eyes narrow on hearing her taking the stairs. "I do this all the time at least twice a day. Now, it was great meeting you, but I really have to get to class." I let her hand go when she pulls away, allowing it this time. I know she has no problem with elevators, and after working as much as she does, the last thing anyone wants to do is climb three fucking flights when you're dead on your damn feet.

"I'm still walking you up." I open the door to the entrance. The keypad is clearly old and dated. Fucking thing probably doesn't work, and if I could hazard a guess, it's been years since it has. Danica grumbles under her breath, ducking under my arm as she goes. "Is the elevator broken?" My eyes sweep the place— peeling paint, dim lighting, and a few of the mailboxes are hanging open. Danica and the tenants here don't deserve this. Rent in New York, no matter the area, is fucking steep as hell.

"Fine," she puffs out, annoyance tinging her tone yet again. I don't reply. I'm too busy following her up the first flight of stairs, hand at the railing when she tosses her head over her shoulder. "Don't touch that." My hand falls away, and I wonder what the heck else is going on in her apartment building.

"Got it," I reply. I'd bet that damn banister is coming away from the steps. Great, now my head is filled with all kinds of things that could happen to Danica. A fire swarming the building, and she's trying to get out without burning to a damn crisp, being trampled on because there's only one fucking entrance and exit. Unless there's a fire escape. Highly doubtful with what I'm seeing so far. I turn my attention back to Danica, the soft sway of her hips as she takes another step, lean body with a slightly muscled tone. It's obvious the woman works more than most others do, holding down two jobs while going to school.

"You doing okay back there?" Danica snickers over her shoulder. Gone is the serious, unap-proachable, hands-fucking-off woman, and in its place is what I'm noticing is a different person once she feels comfortable around you. Don't get me wrong, she's still busting my balls all the while keeping shit locked up tight.

"You think one flight of stairs could wear me out?" We've stopped on the second-floor landing. Her body is still. The backpack she was carrying on one shoulder slides to her forearm. I move closer, whispering in her ear before she can answer, "It takes a lot more than this to wear me out."

"We'll see about that. A man who wears business suits five out of the seven days a week and sits behind a desk all day, I highly doubt that." She recovers after a beat or two, and when she does, I'm out to prove a point. I move from behind her, meeting her gaze head on, and don't bother to respond. Instead, I dip my body, shoulder meeting her stomach, and she's hanging over me, hands gripping my sides, and I feel her small fingers dig into me through the two layers of fabric. My arm bands around the back of her thighs as I hold her in place while I walk a few steps.

"Let's test that theory, shall we?" I goad her when she's eerily quiet.

"I'm going to knee you in the balls, Theo Goldman, but yes, let's test that theory, and then maybe you'll be so worn out by the time we make it to my floor, it won't take much to take you down." Her voice is garbled since her mouth is near my back, so I ignore her need for violating my balls in a manner I'd much rather not feel. If Danica were to use her hands or mouth, that I would no doubt like a hell of a lot more. Since the little fairy has a personality like a firecracker, I don't think my family jewels will be safe anywhere near the vicinity of her body with how she's threatening bodily harm.

SIX

Danica

ALL THE BLOOD IN MY BODY RUSHES TO MY head, and all I can do is hold on for the duration of Theo exuding some weird macho man mentality. Why I'm not more upset than I should be, I have no idea, except he's the first man who doesn't give me the absolute ick. What really annoys me is that my thighs are clenching, my hands are digging into his sides, and it's not to get a firmer hold on him either. Nope, I'm practically copping a feel like a horny cougar, except I'm younger than him, drastically younger, and I can't let a man get in my way of meeting my goals.

Unfortunately, I have a feeling Theo Goldman isn't going to allow me to push him away. We're currently on the last set of steps. The worn step that's been painted over time and time again gives me the clue; otherwise, I wouldn't really know in my upside-down position. My apartment and the building are a steppingstone, sixteen hundred dollars a month for a studio apartment the size of a postage stamp. When you walk inside the door, you're smack dab in the kitchen with its undersized fridge, stove, and sink. The countertop is maybe two feet long, making it impossible to keep anything on the old and aged Formica except my beloved Nespresso machine. A splurge to say the least, along with the pods that go with it. If it weren't for the all too smooth and rich coffee, I'd have a normal coffee pot. I blame Mallory for this current addiction and obsession. The woman is a caffeine connoisseur of the coffee variety and has four different machines in her office at Clean and Gleam.

"Which apartment, Danica?" How, how is Theo not breathless after ascending two flights of stairs while carrying me? Now I'm even more annoyed with this damn man. How is it I get winded after working all day and trudging up the steps, yet he doesn't?

"Three eleven." The only good thing about this place is that my apartment number is the same as a rock band's name I absolutely love. My music taste is not that of today's hits but more of the music of the past. When I'm not working, you can usually find me in an old band tee. And yes, I'm asked to name one or two songs on the musician on my shirt more times than I can count. Theo chooses that moment to move his hands along my thigh in a massaging manner, ruining me further. I'd like to think he has no idea what he's doing to my body, but from the way he surrounded me before picking me up like he's some type of caveman, it would prove otherwise.

"Nice." I bite my lip. Making a smart remark won't have Theo putting me down from his hold. Nope, I'm sure he'd more than likely hold on tighter, demand my keys, unlock the door, and walk me inside. No freaking way. There are some things an almost-sort-of boss/pseudo stranger should not see. My unmentionables that were easier to hand wash and hang dry are one of them, the stack of dishes in my sink are another, right along with my unmade bed. I'm a crazy sleeper, moving all over the place, tossing around like a hot potato, turning counterclockwise half the time. There are actually times I wake up and my head is at the foot of the bed with not so much as a pillow beneath my head or sheets on my body.

"Theo, you can put me down now." I didn't fight him earlier simply because I wanted to prove him wrong on being out of breath and potentially worn out, but the joke is on me because the man didn't even break a sweat. Well, at least from my vantage point, he didn't.

"Are you going to kick me in the nuts?" he asks, yet I'm still hanging over his shoulder. I lift myself up using my hands, wiggling my legs, and still he's relentless in his hold. "Quit wiggling. I'm not letting you go. Not until you promise to keep your knee away from my baby maker." This fucking guy. Next, he'll be coming up with dad jokes, the one-liners only a dad thinks are funny while we're all left scratching our heads trying to understand their laughter.

"If you promise to let me down and not try to barge your way into my apartment." I'm busy staring at his back, wondering if he can even hear me while attempting to lift my body up and over him yet again. This time, Theo allows me to come up. His hands slide up the back of my thighs, then to my ass. When most men would cop a feel, he doesn't. That doesn't stop my body from being a horny little bitch and wishing he would. I really need to get laid. His hands move up, gliding beneath my tank top. Whether or not it's intentional, I have no idea. What I do know is the feel of his bare hand beneath my tank top settling at my lower back has me really needing an orgasm, desperately.

"Thanks for the ride and I guess the lift up the stairs, too," I say once the rushing of blood is moving downward from my head to the tips of my fingers, which are currently tingling down to my lower extremities.

"Anytime. Told you, Danica. I don't wear out easily." One of his hands appears in front of me, palm up.

"No way. You are not coming inside my apartment, Theo Goldman. That's where I draw the line." I go to step back, trying to disentangle from him for what seems like the millionth time today. Theo, being the he-man he is, holds tighter. Good grief, this man is a nuisance to my senses.

"I'm not. What I will do is unlock your door, make sure you're inside and the door is locked before I leave." It's kind of hard to argue with a man who's trying to be a gentleman. So, I do what he asks. I dig through my backpack, where I keep the keys in the side pocket for safe keeping. You never know when you'll need to use them as a weapon, lacing each key in between your fingers in order to ward off an attacker. Yes, I watch too many crime documentaries, another product from hanging out with Mallory too much.

"Okay." I place the keys inside his palm, making sure the one to my apartment is easy for him to locate. Theo's hand is still on my lower back while he unlocks my door with ease, eyes on my own the entire time. He squeezes my lower back, maneuvers me until my back is at the door, and is dipping his head, nose grazing my ear while he's muttering, "The next time you talk about my balls, it's going to be with your hand wrapped around my cock, Dani, and all you have to do is ask." The deep husky tone is anything but joking. I close my eyes, at war with myself, wanting to do a hell of a lot more than have him in the palm of my hand. Luckily for me, Theo backs away, pulls the key out of the lock, holds them out for me, and backs away. It's me who has to regroup. Theo may think I'm the only one effected, but the bulge in his pants tells me he is as well. I turn around, giving him my back, open the door, step inside, then close and lock the door. Theo Goldman is going to make me break a promise to myself, one I never thought I'd come close to breaking.

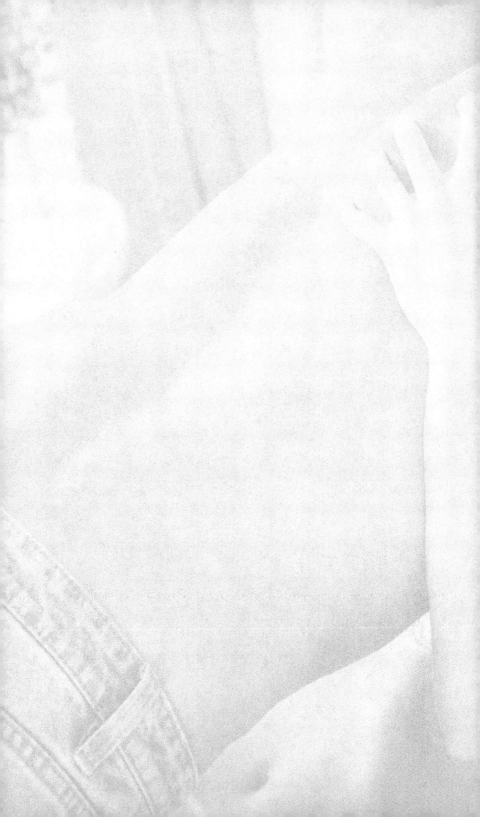

SEVEN

Theo

Danica's door shuts in my face. A chuckle
leaves me, and I stand there for a moment
waiting until I hear the click of a lock. Still, I
remain there for a moment, eyes focused on the
doorknob. Not even a fucking dead bolt. I
already knew when I walked through the
building what I was going to do next. My phone
is burning a hole in my pocket. I'm ready to get
the ball rolling, but first, I need to make it back to
my car. If Danica knew what I was about to do,
she'd really kick me in the nuts, and I'd really like
to keep them intact. My mind is already
wondering what it would feel like to have her
hands wrapped around my cock as she takes me
inside her mouth. Maybe that same sharp
devilish tongue of hers will work its way to my
balls before sucking one at a time into her mouth.
I walk away from her door and head to the stairs
so I can make a couple of phone calls to get the

ball rolling. First to Sylvester and the next to Mallory. I'm going to get so much shit from this. It'll be worth it, though. Danica can't deny there's something between us. Her nipples were rock hard behind the thin tank top and what I'm sure is a barely lined bra. Then there was the way she wiggled in my grasp while I was hauling her ass to her apartment. Did I make sure her body dragged along the front of my body, allowing her to feel what she did to me? You're damn right I did. Danica's breath hitched. While she may have thought I didn't notice, keeping my face and body under lock and key, it was nearly impossible when all I wanted to do was back her up against the door and let her feel what I was capable of doing with clothes on, never mind without them.

"You won't get anywhere with that one. She's an ice princess." I'm almost toward the stairwell when a man talks at me, not *to* me but *at* me. I look at the man who must be talking about Danica. Disgust rolls through me.

"And you know this how?" I ask. The man is propped up outside of his own door, greasy hair, unshaven beard, too-tight shirt that has his stomach sticking out showing more than is appropriate with his unbuttoned jeans.

"Been watching her a lotta years. She's good, real fine, but never lets anyone near her snatch." His crooked teeth appear, yellowed from years of smoking. My anger ratchets up, and I'm ready to cold cock the motherfucker, if it weren't for the fact of Danica finding out. Plus, this damn possibility of a bank merger. While knowing it feels fucking good to use my fists, I also know where to hurt a man worse—his pride, his money, and his self-worth. The one problem with the man in front of me is that he more than likely has none of that.

"What's your name?"

"Brian, the landlord. You?" I take a step forward, allowing him to see who is going to tear him apart bit by bit.

"Theo," I say, "Theo Goldman, and I'll be seeing you around." The lightbulb goes off in Old Brian's head, and I leave him perched up against his doorframe. I'm done playing. Danica will spend her last night in this damn building where a man resides who leers at a woman in a way that has me adding another item to my long-as-hell to-do list.

I pull my phone out of my pocket, hit the code to unlock it, and scroll through my contacts as I make my way down the stairs, double-timing my pace. "Are you calling to bust my balls again?" is how Sly answers the phone. I was going to make the phone call myself to our security firm but figure this would be easier than staying on the phone for most of my evening. Besides, Sylvester is on a permanent retainer. It's only fair to put him to work.

"Everyone is talking about someone's balls today. Jesus, it's like people are obsessed with them or something," I respond, a grin tipping my lips. There's only one woman I want around my cock.

"Man, you know as well as I do that well will dry up eventually. One day, you'll settle your ass down," Sylvester grunts into the phone. I hear Fawn in the background telling him to stay out of my personal life. I love that woman, in a sisterly way, of course, and I'd never say those three words to Sly's woman. The man is ass over elbows for her.

"I need you to do something. I'm at an apartment building on the corner of Amelia and West 304th Street. Buy it. I don't care what it takes, make the purchase yesterday. Then work on updating the building, and get the landlord out of there, too. I don't care if you have to rough him up, send him to fucking Neptune." I can hear Sylvester on the other end of the line, typing away, probably pulling up a website that gives him all the details I'm leaving out.

"There are only two reasons you'd be calling me after six o'clock at night and making me rough someone up. Either they fucked with your family, or you've finally got your eyes on one woman, the woman you claimed never to want."

Sly takes a breath. "We both know your family can handle themselves, which means, brother, you're fucking sunk." He laughs over the phone, eating this shit up. I let him have at it, knowing he'll be calling the rest of our friends and I'll either get a phone call from each and every one of them or a group phone call.

"Yeah, well, if you can shut your trap long enough, I'll tell you all about her." What I don't ask him to do is run a background check. If Danica is working for Mallory, I know she's been through the process. The only reason I had an issue with the last one was because the woman wanted more hours, more houses to clean, and Mallory told her no. Sticky fingers ensued, and she got caught and became jobless.

"Yeah, yeah, yeah. Tell me what I need to know. Don't think I'm not charging you double either. It's after hours, and you're taking my time away from Fawn." I hurriedly give him the information as I walk out of the building, head to my car to sit and fucking wait for Danica. I'll be the one giving her a ride to her college classes, and I'll be the one bringing her home to repeat the process we just went through.

EIGHT

Theo

My phone call to Sylvester lasted until I made it to my car. Danica's worry about it wasn't necessary after all, unlucky for her and lucky for me. I wasn't worried too much. If the car was stolen or sitting on jacks with the tires off, I could easily call for a car to pick me up. Four Brothers has a slew of amenities on speed dial—hired drivers, a private jet at the ready, and houses around the country we can easily use at our disposal.

Now I'm sitting in my car, waiting for Danica to come out to get to her night class while I make the last and final phone call before I'm able to intercept the headstrong woman who's got me thinking thoughts I never thought before. Jesus, Sylvester is right. I'm gone for her, and I only met her earlier today. I hit Clean and Gleam's saved contact in my phone, a personal line to

Mallory in case I ever need something after what happened last time.

"Hello, Mr. Goldman, I wasn't expecting to hear from you so soon," Mallory gets right to the point. You've got to admire a businesswoman who knows how to corner the market with not only commercial business cleaning but personal as well.

"Mallory, I wasn't expecting to call you so soon, either." She makes a humming noise in the back of her throat.

"I hope it's with good news," she fishes, then waits for me to elaborate on the reason behind my call. I can't say that I blame her. Clean and Gleam made a good name for themselves, and if the situation in my penthouse escalated, it could have meant more backlash than she wants.

"It is. Nothing to worry about there. I'd like Danica permanently." In more ways than work, too, but I'm not telling Mallory that. She'd probably think I'm a raging lunatic.

"I see. Well, she doesn't usually clean personal properties. What are you willing to offer?" I already knew I'd have to sweeten the deal. She's a smart woman and would be dumb not to ask for more than I'm paying as it stands.

"Double the pay for both you and Danica."

"She won't accept. You've met her once. I've known her for years now. Money doesn't mean as much to you or myself like it does Danica. She'd rather work three jobs than accept help." I guess it's time to up my offer.

"Alright, double yours, triple hers. But I want her exclusive to my penthouse. Throw in she'll have to make dinner or whatever. And, Mallory, if this falls through, you know what will happen." I leave the rest open ended. Clean and Gleam works at Four Brothers headquarters as well. It's a wonder I've never met Danica before now, though with her weird-as-fuck schedule, it would make sense.

"Mr. Goldman, I'll see what I can do. Clean and Gleam values you as a client as well as Four Brothers. If Danica doesn't agree to the terms, we may have to sever our partnership. That being said, I'll see what I can do." Would I actually severe a contract with Mallory personally? Fuck, yes. I mean what I say, and I'll do anything in my power to get what I want. And what I want is Danica. As for Four Brothers, they'll make us talk it out like a bunch of old ladies meeting at bridge club.

"Hopefully, we can come to an agreement. I'll look forward to your call back, Mallory."

"Likewise, Mr. Goldman." We hang up, and while I'm sitting in my car contemplating how I'll pull up to take Danica to her class, I have an epiphany. Instead of waiting, then talking her into a ride she'll begrudgingly take, I dial another number to place yet another phone call. The damn thing has been glued to my ear for the past twenty minutes, and I'm hopeful this will be the last call I have to make.

"Mr. Goldman, how can I be of service?" Bellamy, one of our trusted drivers, answers on the first ring.

"Hello, Bellamy, I need someone picked up, dropped off, and then taken home after her class. Are you available?" Bellamy is an older gentleman, unlike the other drivers, who wouldn't bat an eye at flirting with Danica.

"As a matter of fact, I am. Text me the address, and I'll head over there right away." The tight-ness in my chest recedes. Gone is the worry that some other male driver will be picking her up. I'm all too aware she'd have no problem putting someone in their place. That doesn't mean I want her to have to deal with more than what she is already. I'd bet her landlord, Brian, gives her more hell as it is.

"Thank you. I'll send the information over now. If you'll let me know when she arrived home. Also, please walk Danica to her apartment door this evening." The promise of a threat I left with Brian may cause some blowback on Danica I'd rather didn't have to deal with.

"That's not a problem at all, Mr. Goldman," he replies.

"There's one other thing. Her elevator doesn't work. She's on the third floor, and conveniently so is her landlord. He'll probably give you trouble. Keep me posted if he does." It's going to take more than a few hours to roll her apartment building into one of our company names that can't be traced back to Four Brothers, meaning Brian won't be dealt with yet.

"Never a problem, and I'll have you on speed dial should something happen that I can't control." This is why Bellamy is a valuable asset to Four Brothers—he's ahead of the game before it starts.

"Thank you, I appreciate it."

"You're welcome." We hang up, and I put my car into *Drive*, taking one last look at the stoop of her apartment, hoping to get one last glance. She's not there. Who is there is Brian, smoking a cigarette, so I make it known that I've got my eyes on him. I roll my window down while driving by at a snail's pace, making sure he knows I'm watching him.

NINE

Danica
___

"OKAY, THIS IS TOO MUCH. FIRST, YOU PICKED me up to take me to school, brought me home, and now you're taking me to work?" I ask Bellamy the next morning after walking out of my apartment and passing by Brian, who made a lewd remark about how he had a way of lowering my rent. Disgusting, vile pig. It wasn't the first time he mentioned I use my mouth to pay for a roof over my head. The problem with kneeing him in the balls is he'd retaliate, and I'd be out on the streets, so my tongue has permanent bite marks from holding back. A few more months before I can maybe be out of this shit hole. What is it with men being sleazy anyways? Bellamy is waiting like he did yesterday, standing beside the back door, car running and double parked.

"Mr. Goldman didn't want you to take the bus or metro unnecessarily, Miss Powers," Bellamy greets me while opening the door.

"Instead, he unnecessarily has you driving me around?" I follow up before sliding into the backseat. Putting up any type of resistance had Bellamy pulling out a playing card I didn't see coming yesterday. I was had. The older gentleman talked about how this is his job, he's made it a career and would never want to leave a woman in a situation that could lead her into danger while walking the dark nights in New York.

"I'd be out of a job if I weren't driving you around. There's no need sitting around on my behind when I could be working," he replies once he's in the driver's seat.

"You're laying it on thick again." He winks in the rearview mirror. Between Bellamy and Theo, the word *no* has become increasingly hard to use. Theo for obvious reasons—he makes me feel free, allowing me to by myself, and the banter between us has me on my toes. Bellamy, well, he's the grandfatherly type who can somehow cajole you into letting your guard down because he's busy looking out for you.

"And it's working," he replies. I pull my phone out to find the last text I received last night during class. It was unknown, and until Theo made his presence known, well, let's say the bottom of my stomach sank to my feet. I'm going to stop this madness starting now. This is getting to be absurd, and while my back and feet are loving not having to walk, I now feel like I owe Theo.

> Me: You have got to tell Bellamy to stop giving me rides.

I put the phone down figuring it's early in the morning. Theo is probably at the office making millions, if not billions, with whatever it is he does at Four Brothers. The four of them made a name for themselves, so it's hard not to know who they are, especially when you have a radar like mine. So, I'm surprised to feel my phone vibrate against my leg.

> Cave Man: No.

> Me: Why? This is a waste of money and his time.

> Cave Man: Either Bellamy gives you a ride, or I will.

> Me: Fine.

Cave Man for Theo's name in my phone seemed quite fitting, and the next time I actually do get to see him, I'll be telling him exactly what I think about his idea of carting me around via Bellamy.

Cave Man: The word fine coming from a woman is bad news...

Me: You'd be right. This is ridiculous, Theo. Seriously.

Cave Man: It's not. You're safer this way. And so are my balls, since I'm not the one driving you around.

Me: For now, they are. The next time I see you, the same can't be said.

Cave Man: Are you asking me out on a date? I accept. I'll pick you up at seven o'clock. See you tonight.

Me: I did not ask you out, you Neanderthal! You can try and pick me up, but I won't be home.

I put our text thread on mute. I didn't ask him on a date at all. How he got that from our very short conversation, I have no idea. I'm beginning to think the man doesn't know how to take a clue.

"We're here, Miss Powers," Bellamy announces. I'm still looking down at my phone. Yes, I'm looking at my text app waiting for a notification to appear yet not alert me.

"Thank you, Bellamy. I hope you have a good rest of your day," I tell him, sliding my phone in my backpack, then I open the door and step out before he can open my door for me.

"You're welcome, and you too, Danica," I hear him reply. Mallory and I are going to have a very lengthy conversation. She's not going to believe how the last sixteen hours went. Crap, I'm still slightly confused, annoyed, and damn it all to hell, a smile has been plastered on my face the entire time, minus Brian. Talk about major ick. I'll bet he's insinuating the same type of favors to other tenants as he is me. God, someone really needs to kick his ass, especially if his threats went further than the ones he's given me.

TEN

Danica

"I'M SORRY, WHAT DID YOU JUST SAY?" I ASK Mallory after I've made my second cup of coffee for the day. Today is only a workday, which means I'll have to lay off the caffeine soon if I hope to sleep later tonight. After work, the only thing on my agenda is homework.

"He's offering double your pay, Danica," Mallory repeats.

"What's the catch?" Theo's balls are going need ice after I knee him and kick him in his prized jewels.

"You only work at his penthouse, Monday through Friday, eight o'clock in the morning until four o'clock in the afternoon." I was going to tell her all about Theo Goldman and his penchant for carting me around until she started off the conversation with a work proposition.

"No, I don't need twice the pay for half the work." I take a sip of the caramel goodness, uncaring when I burn my tongue on the delicious coffee. Mallory has the good creamer, unlike mine at home, which is off-brand and also tastes far less real than what she supplies the hub of her office.

"I told him you'd say that. Theo Goldman is prepared to pay three times your pay and asked to throw in cooking dinner as well." She snickers. My head tips back a laughter bubbling in my chest. I don't cook. If I had let him in my apartment, he'd see that the stove is hardly ever used. My arteries probably hate me for all the salt I take in from the microwave and rare oven-ready meals I make.

"You didn't tell him I can't cook, right?" I ask after recovering. A plan formulates. I'm going to take Theo up on his offer even though I shouldn't. If I were doing this on my own and relying only on Theo's money, I would never. I'm not, though. I have Clean and Gleam writing my paycheck.

"Nope." Mallory pops the *p*. Another role of laughter runs through us, and I place my cup of coffee carefully on her desk so I don't make a mess of my standard uniform—another tank top, this one not white but black, a pair of jean shorts, and my white canvas sneakers. I had no idea where or what time I'd be working for

Clean and Gleam. If it's in the office building after dark, no one cares about your uniform. If it's at a client's home, like, say Theo's, we usually wear a company shirt. Yesterday was a rarity and a last-minute change. The goal was to fix the last employee's fuckup, to get in and out, but the disarray in the penthouse did not allow that.

"So, are you going to tell me why Theo Goldman called, specifically requesting you? Not that I doubt your capabilities. You're one of my best employees and a friend." She's tried to bring me on in a fuller capacity, but my schedule wouldn't allow it. I needed certain hours, and while she mainly works during the day, Clean and Gleam also needs someone on call during the night. College professors won't necessarily allow you to take an emergency work call in the middle of a lecture.

"I have no idea. He walked in on me in the worst position possible, on hands and knees, Mallory. Hands and freaking knees." I flail my hands around, talking animatedly. "Words were said, he mouthed off, I mouthed back, and the next thing I know, we're in this verbal foreplay match. It all unfolded from there. Then I was an absolute idiot and ran into him with a bucket full of dirty water, dropping it at our feet, and that's when Theo told me he was taking me home."

"And you went willingly? My, my, my, Theo Goldman definitely has an effect on you, woman. I didn't see this coming." Mallory has her hands propped beneath her chin, elbows on her desk, and a twinkle in her eye.

"I know! Now I can't even say no to him. It's like he has some kind of spell cast on me. Is that real, do you know? Because it must be. Even his driver is taking me everywhere. Pinch me. Make it hurt." I offer my arm up as a sacrifice. She doesn't take the bait. Damn it, I guess I'm going to have to resort to doing it myself.

"Yeah, a spell. More like you're dick drunk on Theo Goldman's cock." My face flames red. The temperature heating up in her office and the summer clothes I am wearing are not cooling me off. "Wait, you didn't tell me things went that far."

"What? No. Nope. It didn't." I cover my face with my hands, fingers opening a little to get a look at Mallory. She's not going to give up this conversation, so I may as well admit what did happen. "Okay, fine, I felt a very big impressionable presence after he finally let me down from his fireman hold. Remind me to never mouth off at Theo again." I don't elaborate on how he held me pressed up against him for more than a second. His thick dick notched at my center about had me dropping to my knees. Me,

Danica Powers, on her knees voluntarily to beg for a look of a man's cock? Who am I?

"Are you sure this is okay, you working for him? I told him it's ultimately up to you." I shrug my shoulders. Is working for Theo Goldman up close and personal a good idea? Probably not. Am I going to take the job for the sheer joy of watching him eat a dinner I prepared? Hell yes.

"I'm sure, and when or if I have my doubts, we'll talk them out."

"My door is always open. You're also aware that there isn't a fraternization policy in place. Your job is always safe here, no matter what. I'd take that man for a ride myself if I were about fifteen years younger." We both laugh. She could absolutely go after Theo or any other man younger than her. Mallory may be hitting her mid-fifties, but she's still a fox.

"We'll see. Help me figure out what meal I can butcher for him, and then I'll be on my way. Someone has to work around here," I joke. She knows full well that while she might sit in an office these days, it was her who did the hard work for years before she made Clean and Gleam the smashing success it is today.

ELEVEN

Theo

"Honey, I'm home," I announce, stepping off the elevator. My penthouse is usually well kept. Since Danica has been cleaning it, it's spotless. There's a noise coming from the kitchen, so I head that way. Mallory called earlier today telling me Danica accepted the job, but if I screwed up and did anything to hurt her employee in any way, she'd go after my money and my name. I'm glad Danica has Mallory in her corner. It didn't seem like she has a whole lot of good from what I'm learning.

"Hello, dear. Did you have a good day at the office?" Danica's voice is dripping with sarcasm when I walk into the kitchen. She's putting some type of cheese on what looks like a pasta dish with red sauce.

"I did. Is that for me?" I unbutton the sleeve of my shirt. My jacket was already discarded when

I walked through the door. Danica's eyes track what I'm doing, and she licks her lip as I fold the sleeve back one fold at a time. I repeat the process with the other side, taking my time, liking how she can't stop watching me. Her eyes only leave me when I pull a barstool out, sit down, and look at the woman in front of me. Dani is wearing another tank, this one not see-through compared to the one she wore yesterday. It still gives me the outline of her bra, of her tits that are too big for her tiny frame. I want to rip her shirt and bra down her arms, trapping them in place as my hands and mouth feast on them. My cock hardens and my mouth salivates at the thought of tasting Danica.

"It sure is." She clears her throat. My gaze moves from her body to the plate as she moves it across the kitchen island.

"A man could get used to coming home to a pretty woman, clean house, and dinner ready." She places a fork and knife in front of me as well as a napkin but stays on the other side of the island, arms crossed beneath her chest, watching as I take my first bite.

"Good luck finding a woman who would do this willingly without being paid." Sarcasm pours from her mouth, and now I'm thinking about how to put that saucy mouth of hers to good use. Soon, I'll have her. She'll be mine even if she's reluctant at first. I've got no problem using my fingers, mouth, or tongue in order to get what we both want. I tuck into my food, forgoing the knife. No one I know cuts their pasta. Jesus, Italians would cuss me black and blue. I twirl the pasta around the fork, grab a piece of garlic bread she has set off to the side, and bring the bite to my mouth. The minute my tongue hits the pasta, I'm trying to choke down the food. There's not a hint of tomato, garlic, or onion. In its place is nothing but salt. I cough in order not to choke. There's no way I can look Danica in the face right now. She'll know exactly what I think her version of spaghetti tastes like. It tastes like shit. I had no idea you could fuck something up that's this easy to make. It can't be that hard—brown some meat, add a jar of sauce to it once it's done and you don't want to make the marina from scratch, but Jesus Christ, I'd bet my left nut she added a cup of fucking salt. I swallow the bite, using the garlic bread as a chaser since I was dumb and didn't grab a drink before sitting down, and Danica sure as shit didn't offer one.

"Did Mallory fail to mention I can't cook for shit?" she states after I chew the bite of bread that thankfully isn't trying to choke the shit out of me . "Here, drink this." I look up, careful to accept anything from the menace to society in the way of a cook. Danica is smart as a fucking whip, a straight-A student in college, and the same can be said for high school. The preliminary background report shows she's stayed in a women's shelter until she graduated from high school and six months after. It was only when she got a job with Mallory that she landed the apartment she lives in now, and Mallory's name is attached to that, too. Danica's biological dad is nowhere to be seen, and the mother is proving difficult to track down. Her last known address was when Danica was fifteen. I've got our private investigator looking into a few more things, and it wasn't even my idea to run the background check; it was Boston's. Then Ezra and Theo got on the bandwagon after Sylvester opened his big fat mouth.

"Fuck's sake, Danica, a warning would have been nice. I'll tell Mallory to never let you near the stove again," I say after taking a healthy gulp of water to flush the salt out of my mouth.

"You should have asked me before going around me to get what you want. Which by the way, what is up with that? You only want me to work here, nowhere else. Anyone ever tell you that you're a bit much?" she states. I stand up, my barstool skidding backwards. I'm going to show her exactly how much I fucking am. I'll start with my mouth, taking, demanding, and not stopping until she's breathless. Only when she's clawing out of her skin with desire will I take things a step further.

"Oh, fairy, you're about to learn how much I've got to give." I prowl toward her, but she doesn't so much as take a step backwards. There's now cowering away from me. If anything, she's rock fucking steady, nostrils flaring, tits moving up and down with each breath she takes, and nipples showing what she really wants. "I bet if I put my hands down your tight-as-fuck shorts, I'd find you dripping wet." I'm a step in front of her when one of my hands reaches the back of her neck while the other pulls up her shirt. My fingers hit skin, and I feel goose bumps pebble her flesh.

"Theo." Her voice is riddled with desire, her cheeks are flush, and her eyes stay downcast while she watches the back of my hand dance across the front of her stomach, my thumb and pointer finger at the ready to rip the hot-as-fuck shorts down her legs.

"Are you telling me no?" Danica's stomach quivers beneath my touch.

"Theo," she repeats my name, softer, holding the same breathlessness she showed earlier.

"I need a response, fairy. You won't get my mouth on your cunt unless I hear the word *yes*." She tips her head up, eyes on mine. There's a plea on the tip of her tongue, but I won't take what she's not willing to offer.

"God, yes, please." I thumb open her shorts while walking her backwards until she's pressed up against the refrigerator, pulling on the zipper just as quickly. She wiggles her hips to help the fabric slide downwards, and dear fucking God, I'm not prepared for the sight in front of me. I'm on my knees without any pretenses, my eyes glued to her thong saturated with wetness, and I know her core is just as drenched.

TWELVE

Danica

THEO IS DEVOURING ME WITH HIS EYES, consuming me with the whisper of breath he blows over my core, and it's a good thing he backed me up where there was a surface to hold me up. Even if the metal is so cold against my back. It helps calm the inferno blazing inside my body.

"Fuck, I'm going to eat this pussy so good, you won't ever leave." His thumb sweeps over my clit. The fabric is clinging to my wetness, and there's no way I'm ever going to recover from this. Theo won't be like the men in my past—there will be no way I can leave him in the morning light.

"Theo." I can't contain the raspy tone of my voice. My head is tipped down, eyes watching him as he slowly moves his thumb to the side. He doesn't respond. His focus on one thing and one thing only. His thumb slides beneath the band at the apex of my thigh and center, tongue licking my clit through the fabric, and try as I might, I'm unable to keep my eyes from shuttering. One touch, one lick, one taste, and I know there is no way I'm ever going to recover. And Theo has barely scratched the surface.

"Fuck, you taste good. You taste like you're mine." He pulls away from my pussy, both hands gliding to the sides of my panties, pulling them down. The backs of his fingers make my flesh come alive. He picks up one foot. I'd never expect him to plant it on his shoulder. "Spread for me, Danica, show me what I'm about to take." There's nothing easy about the current stance I'm in while shimmying the foot that's planted on the ground to open for his broad shoulders. I manage, somehow, and when Theo dips his head again, he does not disappoint. The flat of his tongue slides out, licking me from my entrance, gathering my wetness, humming while doing so until he's at my clit. He takes his time; there's no rush. Then he repeats the process, a slow buildup that's making my stomach clench, my hips lift up, and my toes curl. One of my hands moves to the back of his head to use his hair for purchase, unsure how I'm going to maintain my stance. The other is flat on the refrigerator, the coolness helping me keep my senses.

"Let go, fairy. Don't hold back." He backs away from my center for a moment, showing me his face, particularly his mouth that's dripping with my juices. He licks his lips. Damn, never in my life did I think a man down on his knees would look as sexy as Theo does.

"Okay." It doesn't matter that I respond—he's already got his head buried between my thighs again. This time, the slow long licks are gone. He probably realized that while it felt fucking phenomenal, it wasn't shutting my head down enough to enjoy the moment, and well, let go. He ups the ante. The tip of his tongue circles my clit, giving me indirect stimulation until I'm gripping his hair tightly. "God, Theo." Reading my body, he keeps using the same pace. It isn't until my legs start to tremble that he adds his thumb, barely dipping inside my pussy, and his lips wrap around my clit. The suction is setting me off, making me lose control. Everything is turned off. There are no thoughts about work, school, how I'm going to manage the next day. All I can think about is the way Theo is eating me. No, he's not eating; he's fucking *devouring* me, and I'm going to become addicted to him.

"Fuck, yes, there, don't stop." My words are a garbled mess, much like the inside of my thighs and Theo's face, but right now, I don't care. I'm not sure I ever will again either. He takes his thumb away, and I feel two thick fingers slide inside my slick heat. The varied motion of his fingers flicking back and forth, the continued sucking on my clit, and I'm done for. My body locks up, both hands delve into his warm chocolate locks of hair, and I hold him in place as I ride his face until my orgasm is over.

"That's one." He pulls his fingers out of my core, wiping one cheek off on my inner thigh, then the other. Almost as if he's marking me with my own cum. When he finally comes up for air, his lips are still shinning and I'm greedy for his lips.

"Kiss me, please." That's all it takes. He's standing up, mouth attaching itself to mine, the back of his hands gripping my thighs and hoisting me up. I'm wrapped around him, arms and legs, as his lips and tongue dominate mine. I taste myself on him, and damn if that isn't hot.

"We're going to my bed. I'm not done with you, not for a long fucking time." He breaks away from my mouth. I only nod, wanting that just as much. And as many times as I can count, Theo is making me forget about every self-imposed rule that's ever existed.

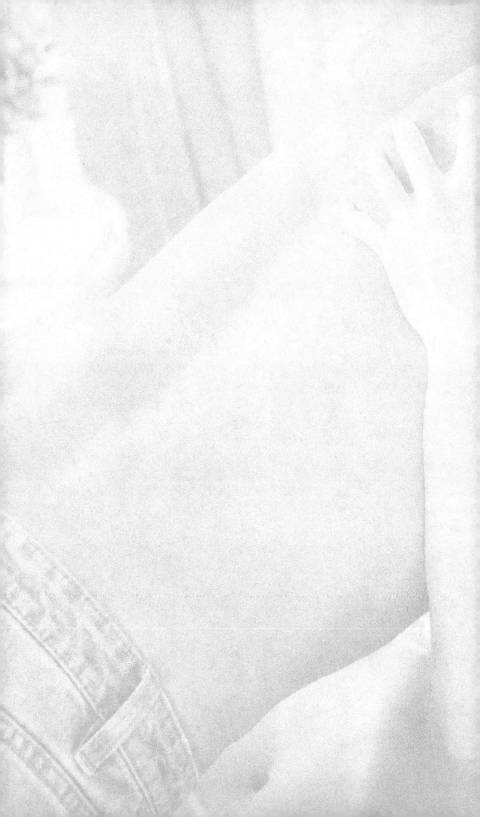

THIRTEEN

Theo

"Fuck, Danica. I don't even know where to begin." On our way to my bedroom, I flicked the clasp to her bra, wanting her completely naked by the time she was where is now.

"Inside me would be a good place to start," she fires back. Her forearms prop her up, her tiny body on display as I take the rest of my clothes off. My little fairy tried to take my shirt off, going as far as unbuttoning as much as she could, but that's as far as she got.

"And how am I getting inside you, bare or a condom?" I shuck my shirt off. Her eyes are glazed with pleasure the whole time. I'm waiting patiently, hoping like fuck she lets me take her with not a fucking thing between us. Never in my life have I asked a woman her preference. I'd wear a condom no matter fucking what, but it's different with Danica.

"I've never gone bare. Have you?" I take a breath. She keeps throwing me for a damn loop, and fuck if I don' like it. "I never have, and I'm on birth control, so if you're okay with it…" She sounds unsure, which is not something I like.

"I'm taking you bare. I haven't either. I always wrap up, and we just had our yearly physical for work. I'm clean." I finish undressing, eyes staying on hers the entire time.

"Jesus Christ, there's no way you're going to fit. Look at me and look at you." She points back and forth. As if I didn't just have my fingers inside her tight little cunt. It's going to take time and a fuck lot of patience. I've got both.

"We'll go slow, and you're going to be on top. This time. The next time, I'm taking you the way I know your body can handle me." I climb up between her legs, stopping to press a kiss on each ankle, then sit on my haunches while I drag my mouth along the inside of her leg. God, what I wouldn't give to slam my cock deep inside her, but she's too small and too tight. Danica isn't a virgin, but I'm thinking the men who've come before me aren't built the way I am. And man if that doesn't make my chest puff out with pride.

"I'm clean, too, and like I said, birth control pills every morning like clockwork." I growl against her thigh, nipping at the skin there before soothing it with my tongue.

"Theo, I love your mouth, but if you don't get inside me, I'm leaving," she threatens, making my smile, and yet I still take my sweet time. My mouth moves to her other thigh, repeating the process, loving the way her body trembles beneath my touch.

"Don't rush me, fairy. You won't like what I'll do in retaliation." I don't tell her I'd latch my mouth to her clit again, sucking the sexy little button while holding on to her thighs, then flipping her over until she's sitting on top of me. That's going to happen soon, too. I want Danica's thighs pressed against my ears as she rides my face, suffocating me with her hot pussy while she gets off.

"Please, I want to feel you." It's hard to argue with her begging me. I move until my mouth is above her cunt.

"One more taste, then you can have my fat cock." I drag the tip of my tongue along her slit, then circle her clit, moaning at her taste. She spreads her legs open further. Whether she's aware of it, I'm unsure, but damn if I don't like it. I've yet to worship her pretty tits and pebbled nipples, so that's my next plan of action. I drag my tongue along the center of her stomach. Her cunt is slick against my skin, and when I latch on to one of her pebbled nipples, she's ripe and sweet, body moving against me. She hooks her legs around my back, attempting to get off, but

I'm not fucking having that. My hands slide beneath her back as I keep my mouth attached to one of her nipples and spin us around so she's on top.

"Theo!" she exclaims. My eyes on hers, teeth nipping at her distended tip before moving to the other.

"Grab my dick, fairy. It's showtime, and you're about to give me the performance of the century." Fuck. My head lands on the pillow, and I watch as Danica does exactly as I say.

"You're so thick. There's no way." Her small hand wrapped around my dick has me struggling to hold back. My fingers press into each of her hips, dying to feel more yet knowing this has to be slow.

"You can do it, fairy, take your time." She uses her wetness to coat the tip of my cock. My control is wavering, and if it weren't for the fact that I've felt how tight she is, I'd have already let loose. She lays her hand on top of mine for support, keeping her other wrapped around me as her knees slide out on either side of my hips. "Fuck, I wish you had this view. It's sexy as hell. Your cunt is sucking at my tip, begging for more."

"Help me, please, Theo." She's not relaxing. Her body is locking up, making me worry I should have fucked her with my fingers first to stretch her.

"Breathe, sweetheart." My thumb moves from her hip, sweeping along the seam of her hip and leg. My goal isn't to tease her, but if it takes her mind off things and lets the pleasure take hold, I'm all fucking for it. My thumb grazes her clit. "There you go. Take me deeper, fairy. Show me how your sweet little pussy can take my cock. I want you to milk me dry." The head of my cock is inside, her heat and wetness searing me. "Take what you can, Danica. Do it at your pace." I groan, on the verge of saying the hell with it and fucking my dick into her. Except she'd be out of commission longer than either of us would care for. That being said, she'll get my mouth whenever she wants. I've got no problem licking her pretty clit until she's coming, soothing whatever pain she may feel.

"Oh God, you feel so good." Her cunt stretches around my cock as she takes me deeper inside. Her eyes close, lips are pursed, chest heaving out a breath, and she keeps taking me, lifting up and lowering down. Man, my fucking control is on a tender hook, ready to fucking break.

"Fuck, Danica. Fairy, can you take more of me, sweetheart? Can your cunt take all of me?" I ask once she's sitting halfway down on my cock.

"I want it. I'm going to." She slams the rest of the way down. I keep working on her clit, her pussy clasping so tightly on my dick. A deep groan leaves me, and I'm done holding back. She fucked up, taking me like she did. I know once tomorrow comes, she is going to be sore. I'll do my best to lick away the pain, but right now, I'm going to fuck her pussy raw.

"Hold on, fairy, hold the fuck on." I move us while my cock is still planted all the way inside. Danica is flat on her back, hair fanned out beneath her, chest heaving, hands going to my shoulders, and a small smile playing on her lips. I've been fucking had. This was her goal all along. "You're asking for it, Danica. You want my cock that bad, to get fucked hard? I'm going to make that happen." I pull my hips back, leaving only the head buried inside her.

"I don't want you to hold back. Give me everything, please." She wraps her legs around my waist, ankles locking at the base of my back, and bucks her body upwards. She fucking asked for it. I slam my way inside her, pulling out and sliding back inside. I'm soaked with her wetness guiding my way and hopefully relieving her of any pain she may feel.

"Mouth," I grunt, dipping my head, kissing her when I hit her deep. So deep that she's locking her arms around my head, sucking me in further. An accomplishment I never thought possible. And when her cunt ripples around my dick, Christ, she feels amazing. My tongue slides along hers, mimicking what my cock is doing to her tight pussy. She's not going to last much longer, and neither am fucking I.

"Theo," she breathes into my mouth, and I let her go. Our bodies are dripping with sweat. My eyes leave her face, traveling down her body until I get to where we're joined. Danica's pussy lips are red and inflamed, flaring around my shaft, coating me, and that's all it takes.

"Danica," I grunt with one last thrust of my hips. The cum leaves my body, and for the first time ever, I come inside a woman. Only this woman means every fucking thing to me. She's the first, and she'll be the last to ever feel my cum paint her pussy bare.

FOURTEEN

Danica

"BELLAMY, I SHOULDN'T BE BUT ABOUT TEN minutes, maybe fifteen max. Please, go grab yourself a cup of coffee." I step out of the car. He no longer attempts to open my door when I get out, though that doesn't stop him from opening the door when I arrive at the car.

"I'll drive around. Call me if something changes, Miss Powers," he replies. I roll my eyes.

"Please, call me Danica. I'll be back." I open the car door and step out gingerly, hoping he doesn't notice the lingering pain Theo spent the better part of the night working my body to adjust to his. I also never made it home last night. Theo had his wicked way with me, a lot. And I'm not complaining at all. The man's mouth is amazing, and he likes using it. He should have a meeting with other men and tell them us women love a man who can use his tongue. That's also why I was not bothered that he ate me before even kissing me. A situation he rectified after my first orgasm. His mouth was dripping with my wetness, and he didn't bother to wipe the mess away. Instead, he took my mouth like he took my pussy. I'm one lucky girl because after he kept wearing me out, ordering me to stay the night when I tried to leave for the second time, he woke me up this morning with my legs tossed over his shoulders as he licked me from ass to clit until I was seeing stars, pulling at his hair, and when I attempted to talk him into taking me again, I was told no, firmly. He went on to say that my pussy needed a break, but he needed a taste to tide him over until he got off work.

My thighs wince in pain as I take the last few steps up the staircase to my apartment. I have enough time to change, grab my backpack and laptop, make another cup of coffee, and stop at Mallory's. I already feel guilty Bellamy is waiting downstairs for me. Theo was adamant that I'd be given a ride no matter what. It was either that, or he'd take me to and from. Fucking caveman.

"A few more steps," I mumble to myself. The last step about took me out. I did notice when I walked in, there were numerous people. One working on the door, another working on the elevator, and another person replacing door handles and adding dead bolts. It was weird to say the least, but these things should have been done eons ago. I swear I'm going to have to ice my crotch and inner thighs when I get back to Theo's, as well as do some much-needed homework that didn't get done last night.

My keys are in my hand, I'm turning the lock, and by the grace of God, I'm in the apartment. A stark comparison to Theo's penthouse, but I'm not playing the comparison game. That bitch is fickle, and I don't have time to deal with her. I move to my dresser to grab an outfit to wear today—a bra, oversized shirt, leggings, and socks. Theo's house is an iceberg of epic proportions, so much so that if I left out a head of lettuce, it would turn to a brick of ice. The clothes I'm going to change into will work for class tonight, too, easy and comfortable for a long-ass day.

I hurry myself along, stripping out of my clothes I wore yesterday minus the panties. They're currently balled up in the pocket of my shorts. If I had more time and didn't want Bellamy to continue waiting on me, I'd hop in the shower again even though I took one with Theo earlier. There's something about being in your own space with your own toiletries that feels amazing. The clothes drop into a pile on the floor, and I quickly slide my bra over my head, one of those that are wireless and comfortable to wear all day and well into the evening. My black cotton thong is next, then leggings.

"Hoodie. Don't forget to grab one," I tell myself as I walk to my bathroom, forgoing my shirt just yet. I've been known to make a mess while brushing my teeth, and dried toothpaste that looks like dried cum isn't on my agenda today. I take care of my mouth, run a brush through my hair, apply some deodorant, a couple of spritzes of perfume, and then I'm out of the bathroom.

A hoodie is on the foot of my bed from the last time I was home when it was a hair washing night. So, I grab that, put my shirt on, juggle putting shit into my bigger backpack, and then do the hop on one foot while hiking up my crew-style sock, repeating the process with the other foot. Sure, I could have sat down, but what's the fun in that? I grab my back, slide my feet into a pair of leather sandals, the dupe to the very high-end comfortable brand that lasts forever but isn't in my budget. Yet.

With my keys in hand and bag on one shoulder, I head toward my front door. Coffee will have to wait until I get to Mallory's. It's been twenty minutes already. I've got to get downstairs. Time is wasting away, and there's a lot to do before Theo gets home. I'm completely in my head, which is probably why I don't notice Brian's presence until it's too late.

"It seems the ice princess has a type. Spreading your legs for rich dick. Figures." I freeze. My back is to him, and he's behind me, thankfully not flush but close enough to cause a ripple of revulsion to shiver down my spine. I'm not in a good situation at all. One wrong move, and Brian could escalate things further. *Think, Danica, think.* What would a woman in your situation do? I really should have taken that self-defense refresher the bar offered earlier this summer. If it weren't for trying to double up on my class load to finally finish, I would have. Instead, now I've got to rely on my memory and pray to God that it's done correctly. Do I try to slam my heel down on his foot or elbow him? All these questions run through my head on a carousel while he continues to talk, "I bet your snatch is tight." A fearful mewl leaves me without my permission. The last thing I need to become is more vulnerable than I already am. Of course, everything else shuts down, and fight or flight hits me when his hand moves to my hip. I'm reactive. Somewhere in the recess of my brain, things click. I tip my head forward then slam it back, right into Brian's face.

"Ouch! Fuck!" Stars appear in front of my eyes. I try to stay cognizant. That all goes to hell when Brian decides to snatch me up by my head, furthering the pain along with my side taking the brunt of a fall I wasn't prepared for. That's when everything fades to black.

FIFTEEN

Theo

"DID WE EVER FIGURE OUT WHAT'S GOING ON with Evertrust?" Parker asks. It's one of the rare occurrences we're all in the office, minus Boston. Unless there's a situation he can't avoid, he stays in New Orleans. Today, Parker has graced us with his presence, which means Nessa must be working the day shift this week. Ezra brought us coffee from Millie's coffee shop, and I'd really like to get this meeting over and done with.

"Nope, still combing through the years. The decrease in money stems back ten or so years, so it's taking our analyst a bit longer." We hired a corporate accountant to work alongside our own. It was a no-brainer to have a neutral party look at everything as well.

"Fuck, this is taking too damn long," Ezra states. He's not wrong.

"We'll go another week, two at the max, then I say we pull the trigger. Four Brothers can take the partnership, or we can grab him by the balls and offer a smaller amount with Trust being only ten percent partner while we have control of the board," I tell Parker, Ezra, and Boston, who's finally joined on a Zoom call. He's an hour behind us and looks like he just rolled out of bed.

"Look who's decided to grace us with his presence," I remark. Boston's hair is pulled every which way, and he's got a cup of coffee in front of him much like we all do.

"I'm still trying to figure out why you're at headquarters bright and early when a certain person spent the night." He raises his eyebrows. It's no use denying it.

"Probably because we can't all fuck off like you fools do whenever your women snap their fingers. You're all pussy whipped." Ezra snorts at my bullshit answer.

"Bitch, please, Danica used to work at Four Brothers cleaning the employee area, yet now she only cleans your penthouse. You're paying a hefty fucking penny. I'd say we're not the only ones whipped by our women," Boston replies.

"Jesus, and I thought Parker and I had it bad. I think you take the cake," Ezra interjects.

"It's not a bad thing, brother. A good woman in your bed every morning and night. Welcome to living the good life." Parker sits back in his chair, looking smugger than ever. I'd like to say we'll get back to talking about Four Brothers and what we all need to work on for the rest of the week, but the likelihood of that happening is highly fucking doubtful.

"Alright, we all good with giving Evertrust a couple of more weeks with the auditors before counteroffering?" I ask, trying to get the hell back on task.

"Works for me. Not sure why you needed me on a Zoom for this. You know my support is with whatever is good for Four Brothers," Boston grunts. Amelie comes around the corner, and his arm goes around her waist, pulling her in. "I'm out. Let me know how things go with Danica and when we should fly up for the wedding."

My phone vibrates on the conference table. Seeing Bellamy's name, I pick it up right away. He's yet to call me when it comes to Danica or anything. A text is usually his only form of communication.

"Hey, Bellamy, is everything okay?" I answer immediately. Parker and Ezra, who started talking amongst themselves, quiet down when they see I'm on the phone.

"No, I'm afraid not. I need you to get to Miss Powers' apartment building right away." I stand up and head out the door, keeping the phone to my ear as I hear him soothe, "It's okay, Danica, stay where you are. Help is on the way." I'm crawling out of my skin. It's going to take me too fucking long.

"Bellamy, I need to know what's going on. I'm heading out of the office now, but I'm still twenty minutes away, and that's without traffic." The elevator opens with a push of my finger, courtesy of having a designated elevator for our floor only.

"I came inside Danica's apartment building. She said she wouldn't take long, but it'd been over twenty minutes." He takes a deep breath then mutters to Danica again, except this time, I can't hear him. I turn around, ready to hit the garage button, when Parker and Ezra huddle in with me, still staying silent but knowing enough not to ask anything, not like I could fucking tell them a thing. "She was on the ground, head tucked between her knees, covering herself, and there in front of her was the landlord." My heart stops. Brian was being hand delivered a message to leave. It wasn't supposed to happen until later this afternoon, once Danica was safely at my place.

"How bad?" My hand not holding my cell phone goes to the wall. I'm worried Brian did the worst possible. Did he rape her? Did he hurt her in a way that will cause permanent damage? Is she sitting on the bottom of the stairs unable to move? My heart is racing, stomach twisted in so many knots while I wait. Jesus, it feels it's been a damn whirlwind, and I haven't been waiting a damn minute.

"She probably has a concussion and a few bruises. Another neighbor called the cops and ambulance. If they suggest she go to the hospital, I'll follow her and keep you in the loop." I take my first full breath since Bellamy called.

"Son of a bitch, anything else?"

"Not that I know of right now. She did a bang-up job on Brian, though. He looks like he went twelve rounds with Mike Tyson." The elevator dings, opening to the garage level.

"I'm on my way. Let me know if they transport her, and don't let her tell them no." I make a mental note to call Mallory and keep her apprised of the situation.

"No problem. See you shortly." I hang up. No other pleasantries need to be spoken.

"What the fuck? Is everything okay?" Ezra asks first. Parker looks at me, nodding.

"Not sure," I reply.

"Let's go. I'm driving. We'll do whatever we need and rally the women. I'll call Nessa as soon as we know what we're dealing with." Him driving is for the best. I'm so pissed off, I'd probably run every red light, graze a pedestrian in order to drive on the damn sidewalk to get to Danica.

SIXTEEN

Danica

"I'M FINE," I TELL THEO FOR THE TENTH TIME since being admitted into the hospital. Yep, I hit Brian so bad with the back of my head I gave myself a concussion. Shit didn't stop there either. I no sooner lost the light when he decided to pull me by my ponytail, attempting to drag me further away from my door, when Bellamy appeared. I'm not sure what would have happened had he not come. I'd like to think Brian wouldn't have taken things too far, but you just never know.

"Danica, you're not. You have a concussion, and they want you to stay the night. In fact, they pretty much said you'd be going against medical advice. You're staying, end of story." I'd roll my eyes if my head weren't pounding. Instead, I gingerly lay my head back, avoiding another conversation I'm sure to lose because Theo, the caveman, called in Mallory.

"He's right, Dani. Please, this once, listen to someone and stop being headstrong. In this instance, it might save your life." I hear the emotion clogging her voice, and I know better than anyone how strong she is. This must really be upsetting her.

"Fine, I'll stay, but stop hovering. Both of you." Theo doesn't listen. He moves my fingers away from the Intravenous line I was fiddling with. Apparently, Theo Goldman knows everyone in New York. Lucky for me, I'm getting the royal treatment. Not so lucky for me, I'm being catered to like the Queen of England. Overkill, to say the least.

"Thank you. Now, I'm going to head out. There are a few people who are busting at the seams trying to get in here, but this big guy is holding them off." Mallory comes closer. My eyes open and blink the tears away. My best friend looks like she's aged ten years in the span of twenty-four hours.

"You're welcome. I'm okay. I'll call later, and I'm sure Theo will text you with any updates." She cups my cheek, kisses my forehead.

"He better, and you better listen, or else." I attempt to laugh. The throbbing in my head doesn't let me, though.

"I will, promise." I nod, give her a weak smile, and then she's heading out the door. Theo takes a seat beside my bed, hand entwined with mine, squeezing it lightly. The door closes softly behind Mallory. My eyes stay open even though Vanessa and Dr Smith told me earlier that sleep is the best thing for me. It's really hard to shut down my brain. I shouldn't be worried about work, school, or the thought of returning to my apartment when I'm released from the hospital.

"Theo." I turn my head to look at him. His attention is already locked on me, gaze never wavering.

"Fairy," he replies, a tired smirk on his face. Theo was at the hospital before I was, holding my hand as they off-loaded me from the ambulance, staying put the whole time until it was time for an MRI. Still, he was adamant about waiting right outside the door. A string Vanessa, Parker's wife, pulled, or it could be the last name or the wing that was named after Four Brothers with the hefty donation they gifted the hospital. Anyways, she stayed with me the entire time, talking me through the process. I wasn't nervous, more annoyed that I was meeting important people in Theo's life while looking like I'd been run over a time or two, put in a situation that had I been on my A-game, I probably could have avoided.

"You don't have to stay. I've pulled you away from work. Your friends are out there in the waiting room, and I'll be sleeping. Go, spend time with them." I'm attempting to let him off the hook. Seriously, my whole life is a basket case. I've yet to tell him the reason why I'm twenty-five and working two jobs, living in an apartment building with a skeeze ball of a land-lord, and why I'm my own worst enemy when it comes to needing a helping hand.

"I'm staying, Danica. We're not going to argue over it. You're not up for the way I'd silence your mouth or the thoughts currently running through your mind." His jaw clenches. The hand not holding my own moving toward my face trembles. Theo Goldman, billionaire playboy who has never once been seen with the same woman twice, is worried. About me. Thank you, social media gossip sites, for giving me the four-one-one while being chauffeured around with nothing to do but scroll through my phone.

"Alright, stubborn caveman," I grumble. It seems being alone won't be an option. It's prob-ably for the better. A pity party over missing class won't help anything right now.

"Caveman? I like that, a whole lot, but, woman, you own the word *stubborn*." The tilt of his lips causes my insides to ripple, thighs to clench, and nipples tighten. I'm sure if Theo took his eyes away from mine and looked down the length of my body, he'd see exactly what he's doing to me with one look alone. Apparently, where Theo is concerned, my body gives zero fucks about a headache or a concussion.

"We'll agree to disagree. Go let your friends in. They've been waiting long enough." I don't tack on that my looks might scare them away. The least I can do is say hello. It's not every day strangers will drop what they're doing to make sure you're okay.

"Fine, but they aren't staying long. You heard the doctor. Rest, and lots of it." He moves in closer, lips touching the corner of my mouth, kissing me softly before he stands up. The softness along with his innate way in taking care of me, it has me melting further for the billionaire I swore I'd never fall for.

"Okay." He nods before heading out the hospital door. I watch him the entire time, his back to me, his shirt a wrinkled mess, sleeves rolled up in what I'm learning is his signature move the minute he's out of the office for the day. Theo makes it to the door and opens it lightly, making sure he doesn't make any unnecessary noise, and stays at the doorway as he exchanges a few words with his friends before he tips his head over his shoulder and meets my stare yet again.

SEVENTEEN

Theo

"Danica, this is Parker and his wife, Nessa, who you already met. Ezra and Millie, Sylvester and Fawn. You'll meet Boston and Amelie once they arrive." I didn't expect Boston and Amelie to fly up from New Orleans, but once Ezra made the call, they were headed to the airport.

"It's nice to meet you." Parker moves closer to Danica, hand out to shake hers. I growl at seeing the IV pulling at the back of her hand with the movement. I take a step closer to stop her when Vanessa slides in front of me.

"Ignore the snarling boy man. Let me adjust the line so you can move around more easily. I'm sorry to say we met under these circumstances, but I am happy to meet you all the same." Nessa works her magic like the nurse she is, even though she's off the clock.

"It's nice to meet you all as well." Danica cuts her gaze to me, silently telling me to chill the fuck out. That's not likely to happen, ever. I've still got a few things to take care of once she's home and settled in my penthouse. The plans for her to have a safe and Brian-less apartment are gone. She's moving in with me, or I'll move in with her. Those are the only two options I'm giving her.

"We won't stay long. Nessa's been here since early this morning, and we need to get home. When you're back on your feet, we'll all have to get-together," Parker states, pulling Nessa into his side.

"I'd like that. Thank you for staying and checking in on me," Danica replies. I'm sure she's telling herself it was entirely unnecessary. Which would be the case if she were an outsider. She's not. My brothers and their wives know exactly what it's like once we claim a woman as ours.

"Hi, Danica, I'm Millie. I hear you're a fellow caffeine head like the rest of us. I own Books and Brews. It's right around the corner, and there's food, good food unlike the hospital stuff they try to serve you here," Millie offers, which reminds me I'll have to see about getting dinner brought up. Danica and I missed lunch. The only reason I know she ate breakfast is because I made it for her.

"That would be amazing. I'm running on one cup of coffee when I usually have two or three. The lack of caffeine is definitely not helping the headache," Danica replies.

"It's nice to put a face with the name. We'll be seeing you tomorrow," Ezra pipes in. I'll be working from her room until she's released, which means he'll be the one bringing my laptop.

"Thank you. It's nice to meet you as well, all of you, really." Danica lets out a yawn, so it's time to wrap this shit up.

"I don't have a superpower like these two, but I'll come and sit with you tomorrow as well. Get some rest." Fawn waves yet stays in place in front of Sly.

"I'd like that. Maybe this one will leave me alone for five minutes." Danica winks, pointing her finger at me.

"Not fucking likely," Sly replies, stating the obvious.

"Alright, you've said your hellos. Now say your goodbyes. There's one more person who wants to see her. I'll walk you out while they talk." Bellamy stayed where he was, planted in his chair. It didn't matter that I told him it wasn't his fault. There was no way of knowing Brian would attack Danica. He still didn't like the thought that maybe he could have prevented it by staying with her. I told him, as did Danica, that she would have never let that happen, even if the elevator was repaired, which it wasn't. The whole damn shaft needs to be replaced and won't be fully functional until tomorrow. Do I wish that Bellamy had made sure she was seen to her door? Fuck, yes. Would she have allowed that to happen either way, had it been me or him? No, she fucking wouldn't.

"Is being annoying a permanent thing with you? They just came inside the room less than five minutes ago," Danica says. I raise my eyebrows. She rolls her eyes. A wave of laughter is carried throughout the room.

"I save my spectacular capabilities just for you," I whisper into her ear. "I'm sending Bellamy in. He's beating himself up over what happened. I need to talk to the guys for a few minutes. Think about what you want for dinner, and I'll order it when I come back." My nose grazes the shell of her ear before I pull away. Her eyes are closed. The woman who was about to start an argument for the sake of starting one is calming down. Hopefully, after Bellamy, some food, and what I'm sure will be another round of nurses in her room, she can get some much-needed sleep.

"Okay, we're leaving. Danica, you're in good hands. Theo has my number." Parker grumbles. "Which he's allowed to use, husband of mine, should something come up, but I doubt it will."

The group leaves, and I squeeze Danica's hand one more time.

"Go get Bellamy. He should have come in with you and Mallory." She isn't wrong, but he was adamant about biding his time. I nod my head in response, then turn to head out with the group, falling into step beside Sylvester.

"Sly, mind if we talk for a minute?" I ask in a hushed tone, not wanting the women to know, though it's kind of hard for Fawn not to take notice since she's right beside him.

"Not at all." Knowing Sylvester, he probably knows where this conversation is headed. The group veers off to right, and I head left. There, sitting by himself, elbows propped on his knees, is Bellamy. He's looking down at the ground with worry cloaking his presence.

"Bellamy." I sit down beside him, my hand clasping his shoulder. "Quit beating yourself up. Danica is doing that enough as it is." That knocks him out of his reverie.

"Son of a bitch, she shouldn't be. She should be proud of herself." He looks up. There's a tone in his voice that means he's back in business.

"Yeah, well, why don't you go tell her that? I've got a conversation with Sylvester that needs to happen." I look at my friend who's standing off to the side, Fawn still with him.

"I'll do that, but when you get Brian in a room, know that I want my lick, too. That girl has been on her own for far too long. It's about time she's aware we all have her back." He stands up after delivering his declaration.

"You'll have your time with Brian, promise. It'll happen tomorrow morning when the girls are here to sit with Danica." If Brian were a man of any amount of worth, I'd hit him where it hurt the most—his wallet. Since he's got nothing, is nothing, well, he's about to fucking become nothing, too.

"I'll be ready." Bellamy leaves me to head to Danica's room, and in his place, Sylvester takes his seat.

"Brian is in police custody as we speak. He'll get out on bond if he has the money. If not, he'll have to wait to appear in front of a judge." He leaves the statement open ended for me to elaborate what I want done.

"Jail won't be enough, not for the likes him. He'll get what, six months, three on good behavior? It doesn't matter that he'll do it again, or me pushing my weight around. Danica doesn't have my last name, and the apartment building will only make it look even worse for her." There's no way I want her to have to relive everything she's had to experience before we met—a judge, jury, or Brian aren't getting that piece of my woman. "Bail him out. Use one of our companies that won't be traced back to us and take him to a building. Text me the time and location. I'll have Nessa, Millie, and Fawn sit with her." I'm not sure what time Boston will be here, but I'm sure Amelie will join in with the other women.

"You got it. One question," Sylvester asks.

"Yeah?"

"How does it feel?" I look at him, wondering what he's talking about.

"How does what feel?"

"To fall in love, fucker. Welcome to the club." He doesn't stick around for my answer. The asshole hightails it back to Fawn like he didn't just drop a bomb in my lap. Damn if he's not right. Danica has me all tied up in knots, and I'm finding I don't mind it all.

EIGHTEEN

Danica

"I'M NOT MOVING IN WITH HIM," I TELL NESSA, Millie, Fawn, Amelie, and Mallory. Never in my life have I had this many people in one room surrounding me. It feels strange yet nice. Theo dropped a bomb on me this morning before he walked out of the hospital room stating he had to go to a meeting but would be back before the doctor made his rounds to release me. I was moving in with him, or he'd move into my apartment with me. Fucking caveman. The next thing he's going to do is carry me out of the hospital over his shoulder. No doubt the only thing stopping him is my concussion.

"Then I guess he's moving in with you." Fawn shrugs her shoulders, a slight smile on her face. She knows that I know that won't be happening.

"It's not a bad thing, you know. We all fell for one of the guys, hard and fast. Now look at us.

We love them, they give great orgasms, and well, we're not complaining," Millie says matter-of-factly.

"Hold off on the orgasms. You'll be on concussion protocol for a few more days before you can have all the fun you want," Nessa says before taking a sip of the coffee Millie brought all of us along with bagels, pastries, and cake pops.

"Don't be a buzz kill," Millie retorts.

"Ugh, he's not moving in with me either." And I'm not staying in my apartment building ever again. Which means, damn it to hell, I'm moving in with Theo until I can figure out where I'll move next, and I'm sure he figured that little scenario out long before I did.

"Dani, you're more than welcome to stay with me," Mallory offers. I love her, but I love her penchant for cats less, as do my allergies. Mal is the epitome of an older cat lady. She currently has six indoor cats, and who knows how many she feeds outside.

"Thank you for the offer, but sadly, I might die from an anaphylactic shock if I stay with you." I went to her house once, and even though she keeps her house cleaner than most, my body said nope, causing me to leave five minutes after I arrived.

"Then I guess you know what you're doing," Mallory finishes, smearing the cream cheese on my bagel. I'm obsessed with any type of cheese, but add cream cheese to the mix, and I love it even more. Thankfully, she knows my love language and has a healthy amount of the white goodness lathered on both sides of my bagel before handing it to me.

"Ugh, don't tell the caveman that yet. I want to keep him on his toes, and I do like to yank his chain." I shrug and sit up in my hospital bed. Millie brought the coffee and bagels. Nessa brought the doctor early this morning saying as long as I continue not to have any issues, I'm free to leave later this afternoon, but he wanted me here a full twenty-four hours. My bill is going to be through the roof even with insurance. Fawn and Sly brought a change of clothes and my toiletries. Funnily enough, my laptop was missing, as well as my phone. Theo must really be taking the no electronics thing seriously. And Mallory, my best friend, turned consort with the man who is stealing more than my attention. He's making me rethink every single nuance of my life, and she's right there egging him on, along for the ride, so to speak.

"Your secret is safe with us," Nessa says proudly. None of these girls can keep secrets. Parker let me in on that when he dropped Nessa off this morning, and Boston smirked because the exception to the rule is Millie. Before we started talking about my issues, each of them told me how they met. Parker and Nessa at a charity event where Parker paid a significant amount for a date, like a whole lot of zeros behind the dot kind of amount. Ezra met Millie at the coffee shop, and he almost screwed up but thankfully pulled his head out of his ass, her words, not mine. Boston and Millie were different. Boston was down in New Orleans for work, became entranced, and they fell for one another. Only Boston's dad is a grade-A douche canoe, and he came home to New York to keep him away from her. When Boston finally returned to New Orleans, he found out she's pregnant. Sylvester and Fawn, well, she was hired to be his secretary at his law firm. Apparently, her dad and Sly worked together, and he's older than her, significantly. The same can be said for Theo and me. What can I say? Clearly, we have all have a type, but don't tell anyone I admitted that. I'm still coming to terms with it myself.

"Speaking of secrets, anyone know how long this meeting is going to last?" I ask the room. Yesterday, once everyone left and food was ordered and delivered, New York's finest men in blue came to question me. I gave my statement as swiftly as possible without leaving anything out. Theo was pissed at me having to recount the events. Then they left. Now, mysteriously, none of them are here. Something smells fishy.

"No idea. When all five of them get together and it's about work, well, it can last for hours. Usually, we'll all go out to eat afterwards. Too bad Nurse Ratchet over here won't let you flee the coop." Millie points at Nessa.

"Please, as if you would," Nessa counters.

"They're on their way back now. Boston just sent a text, which means we need to wrap up talking shit about the guys and eat what we want before they devour everything in sight." Millie takes a bite of the cheese Danish. I didn't realize how isolated I was from the outside world. The world is a lonely place when you only have one true friend—Mallory. It's no one's fault except my own. I chose to stay closed off. Now that I have this group of friends, I'm realizing maybe being so alone wasn't such a good thing after all.

"That didn't take nearly as long as last time." Fawn shrugs her shoulders. She's probably used to long hours and appointments when working with Sly.

"Nope, what, three hours this time?" Millie asks.

"Dang, they're getting faster. Pretty soon, it'll be two hours. We won't even have time to get our nails done without them horning in on our girl time," Amelie adds.

"They better not. We'll have to ruffle some feathers to keep them talking like a bunch of cackling hens," Vanessa mutters, and we all laugh at her description of the five guys. They're worse than most women, especially us.

NINETEEN

Theo

"BRIAN HERE LIKES TO PUSH HIS WEIGHT around. It came to my attention this morning before he was bailed out of jail that this wasn't his first time assaulting a tenant in his building," Sylvester states. This is news to me. Though, I'm not really surprised.

"What are you going to do to me?" Brian asks. His hands are behind his back, handcuffed. His ankles are zip-tied to each leg of the metal chair he's in.

"No worse than what you've done to others," I say. The baseball bat I came to use as a form of torture feels good in my hands. I'd have much rather kept this to a party of three—Sylvester, Bellamy, and myself. That would have never happened with this group. We're tied together in a way where our bond is thicker than blood. All of us grew up in one form or the other watching one another's back. Parker and Ezra in childhood and the rest of us in college. Bellamy has a stake in this now, too. Danica has wedged herself inside his heart like she has mine. Except she's so far burrowed that I'll never let her leave.

"I'm going first, then Bellamy. The rest is whatever the fuck you want to do with him." I toss the wooden bat from the barrel to the handle. It's a shame it will have to be burned along with any evidence that could potentially be traced back to any of us. It's a leftover from my high school playing days. It's worth it to watch it burn right alongside Brian. I take a step toward where he's tied up, ready to take my first lick. It won't be my last either. I pull the bat back and hit him in his mouth first. Maybe he'll choke on his own blood or it'll at least shut him up for a while. This whole time, he's been mumbling some nonsense or the other.

"Ouch, that's got to hurt," Parker says when I slam the bat from the side, using my swing and stance I perfected all those years ago. It turns out swinging a bat is a lot like riding a bike— muscle memory has you remembering what to do, perfectly.

"God, shit, fuck!" Brian mutters after wood met teeth. A few fall out. The rotting teeth will be the least of his problems after we're done with him. I don't stop, not yet. He deserves a few more licks from me before Bellamy has his turn with him. I step back to stand in front of him, raising the bat once again and slamming it down on his nuts. Sylvester didn't allude to what happened with the other tenant or tenants at Danica's apartment building, but I'm willing to bet Brian here used his mouth to do more than talk.

"Oh, this is going to get so much better," Boston chimes in as a scream permeates the air. I relish hearing Brian being in pain. It'll never take over the feeling of not being there when I should have been. I'll never forget the phone call, hearing Bellamy's distraught voice, and seeing Danica in a stretcher. Even right now, in the midst of seeking revenge, I hate that while she's in the hospital, I'm here.

"One more time, then Bellamy here can have his time with Brian." I hit him in the balls again. A groan leaves his fucked-up mouth. The end of the bat meets his pencil dick yet again as my anger gets the better of me. I'm no longer the controlled man I usually am. I take the bat to one shoulder, then the other, going after his knees next. I repeat the process until Brian's head is slumped to the side, his body battered and bloody, and I'd keep going, too.

"You going to let Bellamy have a go at him before it's over?" Sly's voice breaks through Brian's groans and my grunts. The end of the bat is broken, wooden shards in its place, and my hands and forearms are coated with droplets of blood.

"Yeah, you're right." I drop the bat, slowly take a step back, and let my family go to work. "I'm ending his life, though, nobody but me."

"You sure you want that? I can have someone do it for you. It's one thing to beat them to a pulp, it's another entirely to take a life," Sylvester says, making it seem as if he's been in my shoes, and if he has, it'd the first any of us would know about it.

"He's mine," I state without an ounce of hesitation. I'll sleep better at night knowing this piece of shit took his last breath with me taking it all away.

"Alright." Bellamy pulls a pair of brass knuckles out of his pockets. I didn't see that coming from a mile away. The old man has more in him than I knew.

"Fuck, yes," Ezra comments when Bellamy holds Brian by his greasy hair with one hand and punches him with the other. He does this a few more times, showing he's still spry for a man in his sixties.

"That's how it's done, boys. Now it's my turn," Parker states. I watch as he and Ezra do their damage, each of them having a fire in their soul about women being hurt, and for good reason. Parker's mom was abused when he was growing up. He watched it way too often until he could help take control of the situation. Ezra was right there beside him. Neither of them liked watching their mom being hurt. Parker takes the handcuffs off Brian's hands while Ezra picks up the bat, and they proceed to fuck up his hands hit by motherfucking hit.

"Leave his legs for me," Boston says. He's leaning up against a counter, arms crossed over his chest, geared up for battle.

"You fuckers are going to leave me with nothing. I'll take his stomach," Sylvester states, a knife twirling in his hand with skillful precision. It seems Sly has been keeping a few things under wraps all these years.

"Your turn," Ezra says once Brian's hands are broken, fingers in different positions, a few bones sticking out of the skin.

"Fuck, that felt good." Parker takes his place beside me, handing Boston what's left of the bat. My eyes stay on Brian. His head is lolled to the side, and he's pleading, "No more, please. No more." His pleas fall on deaf eyes. There isn't a soul in this room who can save him now. Boston stabs the end of the bat into one thigh, then pulls it out. "Stop, God, Stop!" Boston repeats the process to the other thigh. This time, he leaves it in there.

"Can't have him bleeding out before your through." I shrug my shoulders. I'd give him some Narcan to bring him back to life before I send him to hell permanently. Sylvester throws one knife, landing it in Brian's gut. It stays where he plant it. Another one appears, and he does the same.

"Finish him. This is taking too long as it is. We'll all need to burn our clothes and shower before we go back to the women."

"Make it look like arson. Burn the fucker to the ground. Let me know when the money comes through. I'll be donating it." I don't elaborate. I walk toward Brian, taking my time, relishing in the moment I watch the blood and life drain from his veins.

"You're lucky we made it easy for you. I could have done this for hours upon hours." Brian gurgles, blood coming from his mouth, and I pull the knife out of his gut that Sly used and slam it into his heart. Silencing him forever.

TWENTY

Danica
___

"THEO, YOU REALLY DO NOT NEED TO CARRY ME everywhere. It's a concussion, not a broken leg." I'm not getting my point across, it seems. He grunts but has otherwise stayed eerily quiet since I was released from the hospital. I haven't brought it up, but maybe I should now. "Would you rather I stay somewhere else?" There's a meekness in my tone that I'm not used to hearing, and boy, do I hate it. It didn't go unnoticed that when he returned along with the other guys, their clothes were changed and all were freshly showered, damp hair and all. Nessa and Millie mentioned they like to box to relieve stress after a hard meeting, but I'm thinking it's something else.

"No, not at all. If you go somewhere, I'm going somewhere. You're not leaving my sight." The elevator dings then opens to his penthouse as he whispers beneath his breath, "Not now or ever."

"If you're sure." He carries me to the couch. The normally bright and airy house is currently dim and dark. Theo stayed at the hospital last night, but I'm sure he came home at some point. I wonder why he's got the house so closed up.

"I'm positive. Do you want to shower and then lie in bed or on the couch?" Ugh, this is going to be a long few days. I've been lucky that Theo has yet to see the bruises on the outside of my thigh and knee. Once he does, there's no telling how he'll overreact in taking care of me even more than he already does.

"Couch, I'm sick and tired of sitting or lying in a bed." My arms are looped around his neck, hands playing with the ends of his hair. I take in his side profile, his chiseled jaw, the five-o'clock shadow in full effect, the dark circles beneath his eyes from lack of sleep. Though, none of that takes away from the beautiful man, his warm eyes, full lips, and a wicked mouth he has no problem using. My thighs clench as I remember yesterday morning before shit went to hell in a hand basket.

"Knock it off, fairy. It's not happening until you're completely healed." He reads my mind, or my body, really. I let out an elongated sigh tinged with annoyance because I know he'll stand firm. Vanessa made sure to reiterate the rules after the doctor handed me my release paperwork. Payback is going to be a bitch one day. I just need to figure how to make it work in my favor.

"Spoilsport." Another idea forms in my head as we make our way down the hall. My lips on his throat try to make him fold under pressure as we walk through his master bedroom, which is once again dark. The bed sheets are pulled back, and the light on one of the nightstands is glowing softly.

"A few days. You can wait until then, can't you?" he replies, nudging me away from his neck. I lift away, eyes locking on my backpack by the bench at the foot of the bed. I'm sent back to reality with that blast. Being out of commission in the way of schoolwork for the better part of the week is really going to set me back.

"I suppose." Gone is the teasing, and I'm left with more on my mind than getting off with Theo.

"Shower, then we'll talk." He must realize my mood change. Melancholy surrounds us.

"Join me?" I ask once we make it inside. He lowers me to the ground, gingerly, as if I'm a delicate flower.

"Yeah, I will." He moves around me to open the glass shower door. I work on the knot at my waist of my loose sweatpants. Fawn really went for comfort. She's a woman after my own heart. I pull them down, hissing when my thumb hits a bruise. It's hard to hide it from Theo. "Move your hands. I'll undress you." He drops to his knees, taking one sock off first then the other. My long-oversized shirt covers me from my neck to mid thigh. I will forever be in Fawn's corner when it comes to her selecting clothes—nothing fancy, all about coverage, including the bikini-style panties I usually reserve for period days.

"Theo." I want his attention before he stands up to help with my shirt after my ankles clear the pants one step at a time. "I'm okay, alright? Nothing is broken. I'm here, and that's what matters." Our eyes lock. As much as I've attempted to reassure him, when he stands, pulling my shirt up along the way, it's all for nothing.

"Fairy, you might be okay, but I'm not. Jesus, I should have made it ten times worse." He tenderly kisses my knee where some skin was torn away when I was dragged across the ground after attacking Brian. It takes me a moment to realize what he just said, conveying the reason for the wet hair, change of clothes, and why he was unusually quiet the whole way home.

"Theo, please tell me you didn't do anything that is going to cause us to only see each other during conjugal visits." He continues kissing his way up the outside of my leg, grazing the massive bruise with his lips.

"Conjugal means marriage. Are you admitting that you want to marry me?" I roll my eyes at his remark. I walked right into that.

"No, the words *I will marry you* did not leave my lips in that sentence, caveman."

"Except they just did. It's good to know I've got a chance, at least." He stands up with the hem of my shirt in his fingers. "Arms up." Clearly, he's going to take everything off, which means he'll see my lovely not-so-cute cotton underwear. Oh, well, he's seen me at my worst already, multiple times if you count me being on my hands and knees scrubbing floors. Then my stint in the hospital. This should be a piece of cake.

"I'm serious, Theo. I don't look good in only stretchy clothing, and orange with your complexion is not going to work. Please tell me you didn't do anything that could put you behind bars because of me." I cup his cheeks, having to reach up and on the tips of my toes. Theo doesn't care for that very much, clearly, because I'm being lifted up and set down on the counter. The cold granite causes my body to tense for a moment until I adjust.

"He's gone, for good. I'm not going into detail. You don't need to know anything else. His name won't leave your lips again, and that shit stain will never hurt anyone else on earth." Theo holds firm, staying a step back as he steps out of his shoes, discards his socks, and then pulls his shirt over his head by the back of the collar. Another distinct factor of when he came back: gone was his button-down shirt. A black cotton shirt was stretched across his broad chest, and jeans encased his firm thighs. My panties should not be saturated with wetness, but given the circumstances, they are. This man, who I never thought could be anything other than a billionaire dickhead, is so much more, and he's proving it to me in every single way.

"Okay." He continues his slow and steady stripping of his clothes. His deft hands work on the button of his jeans, the zipper following. "Are you sure I can't persuade you to have some fun?" My hand reaches out when his dick bobs out of his boxer briefs, and Theo does the least of what I expect: he steps forward. The feel of his hand on top of mine, so much smaller than his palm, and his length... Jesus, I'm still in awe how he fit inside me. He guides me as I jack his cock.

"We're doing this my way and my way only." His lips seer to mine while he keeps the tempo of us working together as he kisses me. There's a tenderness while still maintaining a powerful and dominating feel. And Theo is the only one who is capable of me giving in to him so freely.

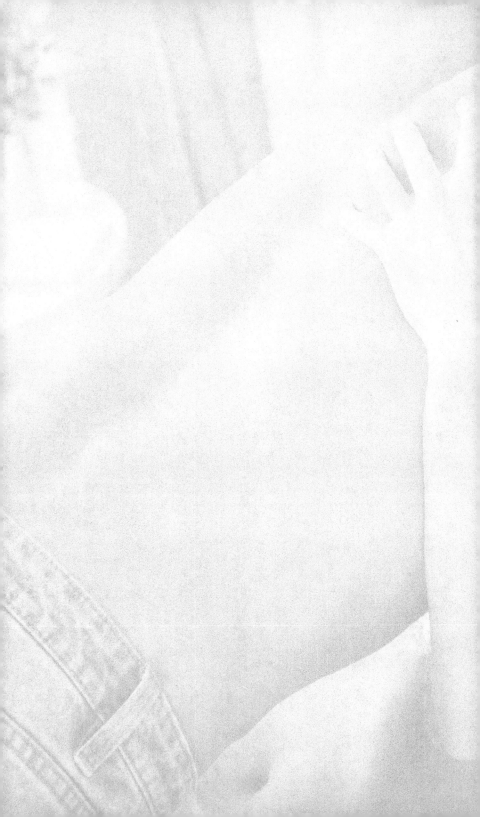

TWENTY-ONE

Theo
___

"Theo, you can't keep me captive here forever," Danica says when we enter the penthouse. She was cleared for light duty a few days after the incident. Since leaving the doctor's office, she's been on a damn tangent about every single damn thing. In the car it was about going back to work, on the way up in the elevator it was about getting caught up on her school stuff. Funnily enough, Mallory is the one who won't let her come back to work yet. I'm not opposed either. I'm fucking relishing that it's working in all of our favors even if my fairy won't admit it.

I hum, staying quiet while she stomps her feet through the house on her way from the entrance into the kitchen. The past few days, I've been working from home, watching over her as she napped or rested. She attempted to fight it for a while but eventually gave up. Her body finally shut down, and she slept. Probably more than she ever has with the crazy schedule she's kept. One day, she must have slept for a solid six hours, woke up, went to the bathroom, ate, and fell right back asleep instantaneously only to sleep for another eight hours or so. A quick call to Vanessa let me know that it was more than normal, that the only time to bring her back in was if her memory started tripping her up. Yesterday, she napped, nothing like that first full day home, so it relieved the balloon of worry in my chest.

"Are you going to respond, or am I talking to myself?" I'm watching her the entire time. She has no idea that while the guys and I were busy taking care of Brian, there were other plans in the works. The apartment building is officially purchased by a shell corporation Sly set up, the elevator is now up and running, they keypad is as well, and new lights are being installed as well as new paint in the main area. There are still a few things left to do, like a new roof, appliances in each apartment, carpet, and painting. Which also means workers traipsing in and out of what would be Danica's apartment if I hadn't moved her out. No fucking way was I going to let them be around her or her things. I didn't care if they were cleared for White House security; it wasn't happening.

"I'm listening, but, fairy, what you don't seem to understand is that I know at the end of the day, you'll be in my bed when we go to sleep and when we wake up." She is either oblivious or hasn't had a chance to really snoop around the penthouse.

"I have an apartment I'm paying for, and I can't just live with you for the sake of living with you." Her clothes hang next to mine in the closet. The drawers in the dresser are much the same. The small desk she had set up in her living room now stands next to mine in my home office. Everything else—books, magazines, and a few mementos—are currently in boxes in there as well.

"Who says you can't?" She doesn't reply for a moment, instead pulls out all the makings for sandwiches—bread, cheese, lunchmeat, tomatoes, lettuce, and condiments. Then she attacks the fruit containers as well. I'm about to make a comment about how much she can fit in her arms when she finally quits picking shit out of the fridge and walks toward the counter. "You're the one saying you can't, when all this between you and me, it's fucking real. I'm not going anywhere. This,"—I point between the two of us—"what we have is not going anywhere, and neither are you."

Danica stops what she was doing, leaves the food on the counter, and makes her way to where I'm standing until her neck is tilted up and my mine is tilted down. Her green eyes are full of an emotion I can't quite put my finger on. So, I let her silence say enough until she's ready to tell me what she needs to. This lasts entirely too long for my liking, us being on two opposites levels. Danica and her much smaller self, tiny is what she is compared to me. More than a foot shorter. The height difference would usually bother some people; it doesn't me. Especially when she has to be on top, controlling how deep my cock can slide into her sweet little pussy.

My mouth waters at thinking about ending this self-imposed torture of keeping my dick out of her cunt this week while she recovers. Now that my conscience is clear because the doctor is happy with her recovery, I'm going to make it my mission to get inside her. My hands grip her small waist, and I lift her up. "Theo!" Her hands go to my shoulders, holding on as if I'd drop her. Fuck, that would never happen. Her ass meets the counter, and my hips move closer until I'm pressed right against her core. The thin leggings are no barrier. Her heat is intense, searing through the light fabric we're both wearing. It wouldn't take much to rip a hole in the seam, and knowing she's bare beneath, I'd loosen the strings of my joggers, bare my cock, and sink inside her until the thought of her leaving me vanishes.

"What, fairy, what excuse were you going to come up with next? Maybe you should look around, the bedroom, the office, the bathroom, and you'd see you are everywhere." I pause between the last three words, letting them sink in.

"Fine, I'll stay." The tips of her fingers playing at the nape of my neck don't convey the words or how she says them. Danica Powers is full of shit, and it doesn't take much to shut her up when my mouth lands on hers. The soft whimper is all the access I need to slide my tongue inside, one hand at the nape of her neck, gently massaging her, and the other trailing up the length of her spine. Her taste is like a shot of whiskey, going straight to my head, and when her body relaxes against mine, giving me the majority of her weight, she's right where I want her—putty in my hands and deep in my bones.

TWENTY-TWO

Danica

"You do realize I went from a woman who worked non-stop to one of leisure, don't you?" I tell Mallory in her office a week later. Why I'm still on her payroll is a question no one will answer. Theo is still in super overprotective caveman mode, taking it to a whole new level. My job? Well, it's basically cleaning the penthouse and going to school if I can't do it online, and, well, I am freaking bored to tears.

"Honey, you were not a woman who worked non-stop; you worked your ass to the bone. Theo and I both want you to focus on schoolwork. If you're that bored, please, for the love of God, take over some of the administrative crap in this place before I sell Clean and Gleam, find a hunky man, and go on a permanent vacation. Hell, maybe the hunk will feed me grapes while fanning me beneath the cabanas." She wiggles her eyebrows. It's then I notice there's a mountain of paperwork on the sideboard when there usually isn't. The office isn't as clean as it usually is either. Hmm, something is going on with my boss and best friend. I can't quite figure out what, but I'm going to.

"Please, I'd love that, and put me on the after hours calls, too. I'm only on campus one day a week now, so I'm available." I put my hands together, literally begging her. Theo wouldn't even allow me to finish my request when I asked. Okay, fine, I pleaded to work again in the evenings at Four Brothers. I relented easier than I should have when he brought it to my attention that if I were to work nights, he'd never see me, which promptly shut me up. This damn man, he knows what to say when I need to hear it the most. He also has me sinking deeper and deeper in the feelings department. It turns out a rich man in a business suit is my cup of tea when it comes to Theo Goldman. The man looks insanely hot in and out of clothes. "Also, what's going on, Mal? This place is never out of sorts." I stand up. May as well kill two birds with one stone. I'm here for the afternoon or until I call Bellamy to ask for a ride, another change Theo and Bellamy were adamant about. I either adhere to the new rules or stay home. It's ridiculous. Brian is gone, and no one else is after me, not even my mom's husband, Charles, worries me anymore. The new rule, though, it's absurd.

Bellamy is to give me a ride any- and every-where—the grocery store, to Mallory's, to Four Brothers. Oh, not only rides to and from. Nope, I'm to be escorted until I'm safely inside.

"Honey, I'm tired and I'm old. So, please carry on with whatever you want to do. How about we switch weekends? We rarely get calls, but I can't leave you with everything. As for during the week, we'll work around your schedule. But hear me now: school comes first. You were meant for big, big things. This business and working for me will not hold you back." She is pulling out the big guns with lots of threats. It's only fair to fight fire with fire.

"Yes, Mother," I tease, moving to the paperwork that needs to be scanned into the computer, sorting through invoices and contracts.

"Don't you start with me. I'm not pissing off my best clients, and you don't need to work yourself to the bone." I look at her over my shoulder. Mallory has a pen pointing at me, and it can't be helped. I stick my tongue out at her before falling into a fit of laughter.

"Get back to work. We can't survive on caffeine all day if you're here to work. I'll order lunch, and you may want to call Theo to let him know your change of plans," she says after we settle down.

"I better. Between him and Bellamy, I have a full-time job calling or texting them my agenda. I'll be surprised if Theo doesn't know my last period, which is due this week coming up. Ugh," I throw out dramatically. I'm going to be out of commission in the orgasm department and miserable. Lucky me.

"Ask Bellamy if he'd like to eat lunch with us. He's the perfect type of eye candy an old lady like myself wouldn't mind enjoying." Okay, not touching that subject, nope, nope, nope. She's like my older sister, and Bellamy is like a father figure. If things start happening then go south, I'm going to have to be Switzerland. I love each of them too much to pick a side.

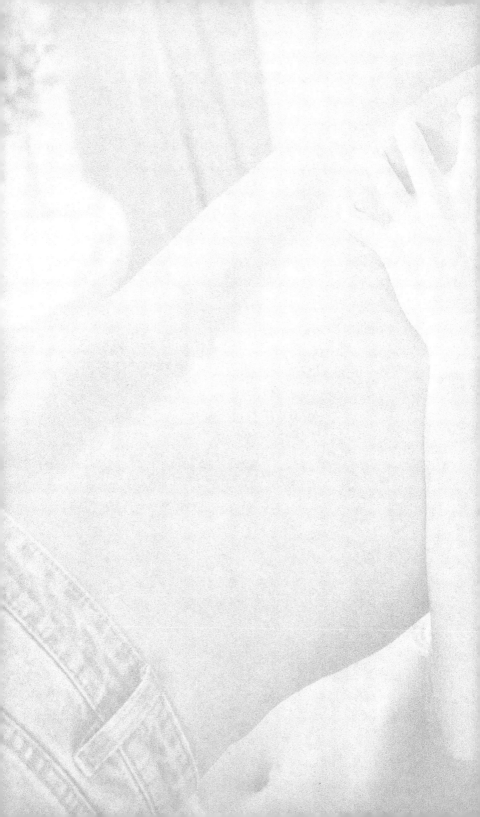

TWENTY-THREE

Theo

"DAMN, THIS IS THE LIFE." I PICKED DANICA UP on my way home after leaving the office. She ordered food for us to pick up, we ate, and now we're on the couch.

"Just don't expect me to actually cook." She nestles closer to me, head on my chest, hand on my lower abdomen. My arm is around her shoulder, and I'm slowly massaging her head with the tips of my fingers. Our food lies abandoned on the coffee table, annoying Danica. She likes to keep things picked up and clean. The only way to keep her seated and where she's at is keeping up with the ministrations of working my magic. Her throaty moan is all the answer I need.

"Fairy, you don't ever have to attempt to cook again. I'd prefer it, really." She lifts up off my chest, a look of irritation on her face.

"I can cook. Well, let me rephrase that. I can heat food up and make an awesome salad." I grimace at the thought of a salad every day for dinner or heating something up from the freezer department in the grocery store.

"Is there a reason you can't cook?" We haven't touched a whole lot on her past as in before she met Mallory, and I know Mal cooks. Bellamy gave me that piece of information today. It seems the two of them are getting close as of recently.

"I used to bake with my mom. It was our thing on Sundays." She shrugs her shoulders, and I figure that's all I'll get out of her, but I'm unprepared for the emotional dumping that continues. "That was before she met her now husband, before things changed. Gone was the mom who worked six days a week yet somehow managed to be there for every fair, dance, and award ceremony. One day, she came home, announced that she met a man, and they were getting married. I'd never met the guy or knew she was dating. That goes to show you just how sneaky we as human beings can be." She takes a deep breath. "We moved, uprooted from our small apartment into a monstrosity of a house, bigger than your penthouse and some of the other places I've cleaned. The first year was okay. I kept to myself, got phenomenal grades, worked at a grocery store. Anything to stay out of the McMansion. It wasn't until Charles started making weird comments, talking about how he had a few colleagues who wouldn't mind a pretty little thing like me. I was done, he yelled, I packed my bags and grabbed what cash I had, which wasn't a lot since I was an eighteen-year-old girl still in high school for a few more months." She closes her eyes. One lone tear slides down her cheek. My thumb catches it. I hate that she's hurting. I'm seething inside for the man who made her feel like she had no other choice but to leave. And her mom… Who the fuck would put their flesh and blood in a situation like this?

"Fairy, Jesus Christ." My forehead meets hers. Her green eyes are filled with hurt, and I'm ready to slay another motherfucker.

"It's okay. I got out. My mom, she ran after me. I begged her to come with me, but she wouldn't, and while that sucked, Mom did what she could. She gave me a wad of cash and her love." She faceplants into my chest. Both of my arms wrap around her as she cries quietly. I don't say anything. Right now, she doesn't need words. I have a feeling Danica never let herself feel or speak of what happened all those years ago. I'd also bet there's way more to the story than she's telling me, but I'm not going to push. One thing about Danica is that she holds it in, not saying a word until she's damn good and ready.

"Come here, fairy." I pick her up until I've got her where I want her—ass in my lap, her arms looped around my neck, and her nose in the crook of my neck.

"He was hurting her, Theo. There were bruises, and she was staying to protect me. I didn't know it then, but I do now. Why else would she say she couldn't come with me?" she mutters into my skin. My hand slides beneath her shirt, where I rub her back up and down as my other gently combs through her hair, trying to soothe her.

"Have you seen her since that night?" I ask, prodding. It isn't the time or the place, but that doesn't mean shit. Not when I can fix this for her. Between Sylvester and Four Brothers, it won't take much.

"No, I've been too scared to. I know she's alive and have seen her from a distance, but other than that, no." She lifts off my chest and cleans up the tears she shed with the backs of her hands, a weak smile in place. "I'm sorry about breaking down on you. Wow, it's been a long time since I have let myself think about my mom. There was never enough time, and I knew if I did, I'd have a hard time recovering by myself."

"You're not on your own anymore, and you never have to apologize to me, not ever, Danica. I'm here, always. I'm assuming this stepdad is the reason why you hated me at first glance?" I rub my hand up and down her back, scratching it every two or three passes.

"You're right, which wasn't and isn't fair to you. I shouldn't have lumped you in with the likes of Charles Trust." The breath she lets out is one of relief. "I'm sorry."

"What did you say?" I ask, making sure I heard her correctly even though my ears have never deceived me.

"I'm sorry. I know those words are hard to imagine coming from me," she laughs it off.

"Not that. Did you say Charles Trust? The wealthy grandson to EverTrust Banking?"

"Yep, that would be him." It takes a lot to lock my shit down. My molars are going to be ground down to shit from trying to maintain a semblance of normalcy. "Why? What's wrong? Theo, I swear to God, if you do something stupid to take you away from me, prison won't be enough." I chuckle, hating like hell I'm about to make a phone call and ruin our quiet night at home.

"I'm not making a promise I can't keep, but I'll tell you this. I'd do anything for the woman I love, and if that meant living behind bars to keep you safe, then so fucking be it." Not the best way to admit you love your woman for the first time.

"I love you, Theo Goldman, suit or no suit, money or no money. An orange jumpsuit is yet to be determined, but I'll bring you a nail file in a cake."

"I love you, fairy, and as much as I want to relish in this moment and take you to bed, we're about to be invaded. I've got to make a call that can't wait. Trust came to us, looking for a partner. Nothing is signed yet. We're still in the preliminary process, but this can't wait," I tell her the truth.

"I'm beginning to think I'm part of the problem in this relationship. I mean, this one kind of came out of left field, but still. Can't our lives be boring for a week or so?" she asks.

"Fairy, our life is anything but boring. Now, kiss me before the chaos rains down on us." That gets her attention. Her lips land on mine. I nip at them until she opens for me, and then my tongue is inside, gliding against hers, giving her a taste of what my mouth is going to do later tonight: Danica naked, legs spread, and my shoulders wedged between her thighs.

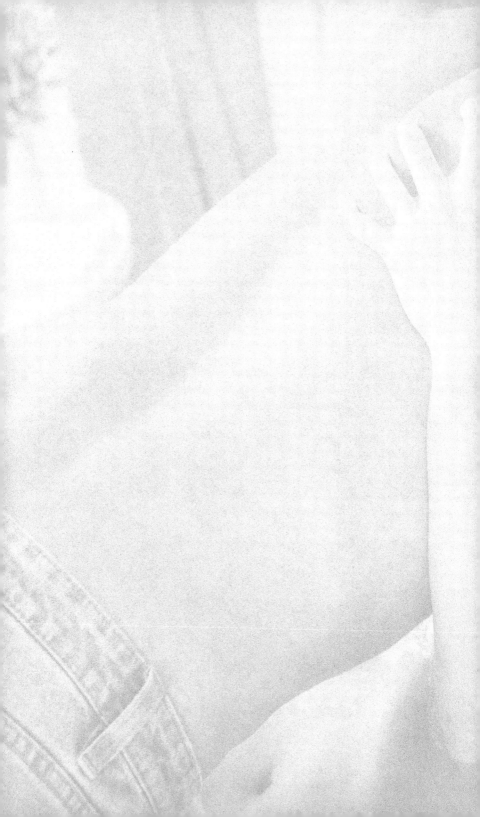

TWENTY-FOUR

Theo
___

"JESUS, I'M CHARGING TRIPLE," SYLVESTER greets me once he's inside my home office. Parker and Ezra are already here. The fuckers are enjoying a good bottle of bourbon. Boston is back in New Orleans. We'll catch him up to speed tomorrow when we're back in the office.

"I'd expect no less. Fucking lawyers," I joke as I sit down on top of my desk, facing the two chairs. Sly takes the vacant seat. Ezra likes to stand when we talk shit out. He's got ants in his pants, and right now, he's got his gaze one Danica's desk.

"How very domesticated of you, Theo." I'd expect nothing less from my friends. I gave them hell for falling fast and hard for their women. Now look at me.

"Very funny. It's your wife who takes over your office, right? At least I share mine," I grunt out my response.

"Alright, let's get down to brass tacks. I hate dragging Nessa out of the house this late when she has to work tomorrow morning." Vanessa must still be on days. I'm sure Parker is more than pleased with her schedule. Though, we're a lot alike in the fact that we'd be happier if they stayed home and didn't have a job. Maybe I am a caveman like Danica says after all.

"Whatever we we're planning to do with Ever-Trust is off the table. I'm pulling rank this time around. I know we did a lot for everyone in this room, myself included. Charles Trust is Danica's stepfather and the reason she left home when she was eighteen." I let my words sink in, waiting before I elaborate.

"Motherfucker. What do you mean the reason she left?" Sylvester's intense stare is locked on me.

"Shit, do whatever you need to. We don't need a bank that'll be more of a headache than we need," Ezra states.

"Is this going to turn into the same situation as last time? Because if so, I'm in," Parker suggests. He's bloodthirsty when it comes to men hurting women.

"I'm told it better not because conjugal visits, orange jumpsuits, and sending nail files aren't on Danica's to-do list." The guys get a kick out my response. "Anyways, she left at eighteen, has her biological father's last name, and a friend of Mallory's was willing to seal her file after she made it to the women's shelter. That's why when we ran Charles boy's name, there was no hit on him regarding Danica." Once I made the calls to the men in this room, Danica elaborated a bit more. She even talked about the bruises and how the lights went out in her mom's eyes the night she left. My woman is strong, a lot fucking stronger than any one person should ever have to be. "Charles didn't have a chance to get his hooks in Danica. Though, given the opportunity, I'm sure he would have. His comments caused her to lock her bedroom door with a chair beneath for good measure, and she had a go-bag on the ready, which told me plenty. It's the fact he brought his associates around that really got me thinking." I take a healthy sip of my own bourbon.

"So, he's another man willing to use his authority for his own gain." Sylvester has one foot over his knee, frustration laced through his tone.

"Yep, Mrs. Trust was and is his current victim. Danica said her mom had bruises on her when she left. She goes around once or twice a year, stays hidden while getting a glance at her mom, but she is too scared to approach."

"I guess this is all adding up on how we couldn't figure out where EverTrust's money was going. I'm willing to bet he's funneling it out to pay his associates for whatever they want," Ezra says what I've been thinking since putting things together.

"Well, for obvious reasons, the contract and merger are null and void," I tell them.

"Abso-damn-lutely," Ezra agrees. Parker nods his response. We're all on the same page.

"The next question is how to proceed?" Sly asks, but I can see the wheels are turning in his head like all of ours surely are.

"Dismantle him piece by piece, figure out who his associates are, and start exposing them," I say without a hint of remorse. "If Boston were here, he'd say the exact same thing. Make it so it won't come back on Sly's firm or Four Brothers. It'll be easy to get out of any contract with him, now more than ever. I only ask that you keep Danica's name out of it. If that means I hang back and don't come into Four Brothers for a while, so be it." That'll be harder on Parker and Ezra, more Parker with his penchant of working from home. Ezra comes in more but not every day like I do.

"We'll figure it out. Right now, we're all heading home with our women. We'll call Boston in the morning, apprise him of the situation. Sly will have to do work more than all of us as soon as he figures out a safe and smart way to disassemble him from the inside out. Let them turn against one another," Parker wraps our impromptu meeting up, simultaneously suggesting to Sylvester how to start dealing with this situation.

"Theo, glad to see you're happy, brother. It's about damn time. Can't wait until there are little Danicas running around the penthouse," Ezra jokes as he shakes my hand after we all head out my office door.

"Take that shit back. The woman busts my balls at least nine times a day. Christ, if we have girls with her beauty and attitude? I'm fucked, completely fucked." Children with Danica hadn't crossed my mind yet. We've been too busy dealing with one damn catastrophe after the other. Now that it has, I'm wondering if I can somehow throw her birth control pills in the trash without her noticing. Highly unlikely. It doesn't matter if she's in the hospital, recovering from a concussion, or working two damn jobs. She never forgets to take them, ever.

"This is going to be fun to watch," Ezra finishes off before we reach the mouth of the hallway. The girls have popcorn, chips, drinks, and what looks like desserts surrounding them while a reality show plays on the television. It doesn't matter that we're in a high-rise penthouse that's worth billions and has panoramic million-dollar views. Our women are creatures of comfort—good food, good company is all they really need or want.

TWENTY-FIVE

Danica

"SO, ARE YOU GOING TO TELL ME WHAT THE menfolk talked about?" I ask Theo. I've held my question in long enough. Of course, it was me who was craving a long hot shower, needing to decompress after pouring out years of pent-up emotion. And what does that say about myself? I cried over my mom, but the Brian situation? Not so much. I was more pissed off than anything, but also too out of my mind to do anything except retaliate. Theo taking care of him in a way that no judge, jury, or prosecutor can also helped. Yep, that's how little faith I have in our system, especially when Theo elaborated about Brian's past. It also helped that he made sure he was there while I recovered and anytime I needed to talk it out or replay what happened. Some of those times were tense, for me and Theo. Now I'm out of the shower, and the stress and worry are still at the forefront of my mind. Which is why I'm asking what they're planning in a roundabout way.

"You know, the normal. Women, marriage, and babies." My eyes must pop out of my head judging by the deep chuckle I'm met with. I'm standing at the foot of the bed wrapped in a towel, and Theo is wearing nothing but a pair of jeans. The look in his eyes is telling me I'm going to be his next meal, and I'd willingly have thrown myself at him, too, if it weren't for the babies comment.

"Hold your horses there, big guy. No babies are coming out of me anytime soon." I step back. Theo moves closer, and when the back of my knees meet the mattress, he continues his slow perusal of my body, starting at the bottom and working his way up. The searing of his eyes causes my thighs to clench. Theo is a man of many talents, but his mouth, Jesus, he uses it in a way that has me seeing stars, calling him my god, and begging for him to stop after one orgasm rolls into another.

"Hmm, I wonder if I could make you change your mind. Tell me, Danica, would you carry my kids, your stomach swollen with our child?" His hand tugs at the end of my towel. One tug, and it's on the ground, leaving me bare.

"Theo." My mind blanks, my worries fading away when he unbuttons his jeans and they drop from his waist, his hard cock pointing upwards along his lower abdomen.

"Answer me first. Then you can have your choice of my mouth or my cock." One of his hands cups my breast, thumb sliding over my nipple. I watch as his fingers grip his thick shaft. His hands are much larger than mine, and still, the tips of his fingers barely meet. He twists his wrist with every upward and downward stroke. My mouth goes dry, and I whimper with wanting to drop to my knees and choke on his dick. "Fairy, answer the question." He moves closer.

"Yes," I admit. Never in my life did I think I'd have the chance, let alone a man who would love me as completely as Theo does. Yet here he is, offering more than I could have ever expected.

"When?" He releases his cock and wraps his arm around my lower back, and then we're both going down together. My back meets the mattress, thighs spreading willingly for him to invade more than my body. Theo invades my heart and soul, too.

"You're not playing fair," I groan, hips arching up, legs hooking around his lower back, ankles locking together.

"I never said I would. Tell me. When am I throwing away your birth control pills?" He drags the underside of his length against my slit, further escalating my desperation to feel him inside me.

"Not right now." My body tenses when I feel his thick mushroom-shaped tip inside my pussy. He doesn't move, holding himself steady as I clench around him, both of us relishing how we feel together.

"I need more than that, fairy." I don't know if he's talking about his cock inside me or a better response. Either way, I'm unable to string two words together, let alone answer in a way he'll be content to hear.

"Theo," I say on a long groan when he takes his cock away. His hands grip the backs of my thighs, holding them there as his head dips between my legs. Theo's wide and wet tongue strokes the length of my center. All I'm left to do is watch as his head moves up and down, keeping the pace slow and teasing my clit with every pass.

"I'm giving you three months, that's it, Danica. Then my cum is going to stay inside you, unprotected." He lifts his head. My wetness coats his lips. He licks at them as he makes a statement, I know he'll hold on to.

"Fine," I relent when he shows no signs of going back to feasting on my needy pussy. The smile that takes over his features should be illegal.

Theo Goldman knows exactly what he's doing to me, persistent in his task to get what he wants.

"Good answer." He goes back to eating me like I'm his last meal. One finger slides inside my pussy, another along my ass. Pleasure like never before takes ahold of my nerve endings. I'm moaning his name while one hand fists the back of his head, holding him in place, my other clenching the sheets. My body convulses as Theo continues his slow and steady pace. He likes to slowly build up my orgasm before pushing me over, and tonight, I have a feeling the second I'm coming, he's going to slam his cock inside me only to build me back up all over again.

"Yes, there, please don't stop," I beg, eyes slamming shut, body locking up so tightly my muscles hurt. Theo doesn't stop. He's in it to win it, and I'm reaping the rewards.

TWENTY-SIX

Theo

"FAIRY, WAKE UP." I KISS HER BARE SHOULDER.
We were both worn out last night after everyone
left. Shit, my dick is about drained fucking dry,
and while we both needed it after she let everything out, I didn't expect her to sleep through
my phone ringing, me getting out of bed, taking
a shower, and even right now. This woman is
sleeping the damn morning away. The call I just
got off with Sylvester means it's time for her to
know the game plan. The only problem is,
Danica is somehow sinking deeper into sleep.
I'm about to slip the sheet and comforter off her
body when she finally starts moving.

"I'm sleeping. Either get in or pull the sheet up.
I'm cold." She shivers before cuddling further
into my abandoned pillow. I smile. My, my, how
things have changed within the last few weeks.
At one time, she was doing everything she could

to keep me at bay. Now she wants me closer. Fuck, but I love this woman.

"You can't do either." I slide my hand beneath the sheet. I'm met with soft skin. It also does the trick because where she's been warm and under the sheets, my hand is cool to the touch.

"Theo Goldman, I'm going to murder you." She flops onto her back, tucking the comforter with her, obscuring her bare body from my view. "I'm awake now, and you're a cruel, cruel man."

"If you murder me, who will give you the orgasms you crave?" I tease her, moving until I'm on top of her, boxing her in with my forearms on either side of her head. Her face is still soft from sleep, eyes glassy, and lips still plump from my mouth on hers throughout the night.

"Bob. He worked before you. I'll use him again." Her quick-witted response before caffeine is uncanny.

"Is that so? I guess you won't need this again?" I dip my hips. Her legs open for me through the sheets, and with her sharp intake of breath, Danica's body tells me what her voice doesn't.

"Come on, sleepy head, I'll make you a cup of coffee while you get out of bed." My lips graze hers twice before I finally move away from her. I swear she's like oxygen to my lungs—it's impossible to breathe without her nearby.

"Fine, but I want breakfast, too." She pouts her lips as she sits up in bed, still not getting out.

"Demanding little fairy this morning," I reply. I'll more than likely have to come back in here to wake her up again. She is taking to working in the office and at home better than expected. It also means she's able to keep a normal schedule and sleep until eight or nine o'clock. When she was working before, she was up at six after only getting into bed at midnight, sometimes one.

"Bagel and cream cheese, please." Not an ounce of protein for breakfast. The woman runs on caffeine, cheese, and carbs.

"Get your ass moving, or it won't happen." She huffs out an exaggerated puff of air, but I don't stick around. If I did, neither of us would be leaving the bedroom for the foreseeable future.

"Don't forget the extra cream cheese!" she calls out behind my back. I shake my head. One day, she'll eat an omelet with some vegetables, but until then, it looks like I'm going to buy stock in cream cheese. It doesn't take me long to get to the kitchen. The coffee brewer is already on from making my own while Sylvester was on the other end of the line. Instead of us all heading into the office, we settled on a conference call as he laid out what wasn't hard to uncover. Ever-Trust is so in the red, there's no way we'd have touched it in order to turn it around. The associates Charles spoke about within his own company, they weren't much better, funneling money in and out of EverTrust, laundering whatever they could without getting caught. Shit is going to come crashing down in the next day or so. It's time I prepare Danica for the fall.

I throw a pod in the one-cup brewing system—caramel flavor—and put her preferred coffee mug she gravitates to on the daily. Then grab the creamer out of the fridge along with the cream cheese, setting it on the counter, and only when I'm working on toasting her bagel does she grace me with her presence.

"I take it back. I'm not going to murder you," she says, wearing my shirt from yesterday, hair in a messy bun and voice thick with sleep.

"It's my impeccable demeanor, isn't it?"

"Yeah, right. Dragging me out bed this early, I'm going with orgasms and that you can cook." She adds her sugar while I push the bagel down in the toaster.

"Fairy, we both know it's the full fucking package." I wrap my arms around her from behind as she takes a sip of her coffee. "Fucking sucks I've got to ruin our morning, but Sylvester is finding a wealth of information, and I want to prepare you." It seems like there's always some kind of corruption whenever there's money involved. I'm not saying taking a life is a good thing, but my moral compass is fucking skewered when it comes to Danica. There are men who deserve to die and men who deserve to rot in prison. Prison was too good for Brian. Air to breathe was too great a gift for the likes of him. As for Charles, taking away his money, a free life, and being known as an abuser, well, that's a whole other story.

"Okay, let's do this." She turns around, and I lift her up until she's sitting on the countertop. "Man, my ass always takes the brunt of you picking me up," she jokes.

"Make your bagel while I talk." The bagel pops up, and I plop it on a plate, grab the knife and cream cheese, then slide it on the counter nearest to her thigh.

"Okay, caveman." She rolls her eyes but gets to work while I make myself another cup of coffee.

"Sylvester found the weakest link among them. Shit is happening, and it's going to happen fast. Each of the guys who were in on a not-so-complicated money laundering deal are ratting each other out left and right. It's only a matter of time until the media gets ahold of it, which means I need to know what to do about your mom." The bite of bagel she was about to take after she smothered and covered it with cream cheese is held out in front of her. The slew of emotions crossing her face has me worried. Maybe this is too much too fucking soon. It helped that Four Brothers and Sylvester have an auditor in place. A few key links from Danica, and shit happened fast.

"Make sure she's safe. Please don't let Charles hurt her. Not anymore."

"Done. I'll set her up. We've got houses where she'll have a soft place to land, and I'll get her an untraceable phone. Anything else?" She shakes her head. I pluck the bagel from her hand, drop it to the plate, and my hands cup her cheeks. "Everything is going to be okay, I promise you." Her eyes close, our foreheads meet, and her arms band around my waist. I let her have her moment. When she's ready, she knows this is where I'll be. Always by her side no matter what.

TWENTY-SEVEN

Danica

"THEO?" I ASK THROUGH THE OPEN DOORWAY leading from the living room to the outdoor area. It's two days after he told me their plan was in place. He was true to his word, and Theo and his friends—well, my friends now, too—their wives included, rallied. Apparently, I'm not the first woman in our group to need help. I'm hopeful I'll be the last. These guys have done more than enough for me, and I have no way of paying them back. Though, I'm sure even if I could, they wouldn't allow it.

"I take it things went well?" he asks, stepping outside. I stand up from my chair and walk toward him, my head nodding rapidly like I'm a bobble head figurine.

"Yeah, she wants to see me, and I want to see her, too." I look up at him, my neck craning as I wrap my arms around his waist. One of his hands slides beneath my hair, fingers going to the base of my neck and working their magic.

"I want that for you, but we need to make sure the dust settles. Let the district attorney do their investigating. The last thing any of us want is to think she had anything to do with Charles and EverTrust with the bullshit that keeps coming to light." The money laundering was the tip of the iceberg. Charles and his associates were also luring young men and women into the lion's den. They'd come up with some kind of made scheme, telling them if they didn't do what they said, they'd make their lives and their families' lives a living hell any way possible. Financially, politically, and sexually. Preying on the innocent. They're sick, sick people, and I'm so glad they're getting what they deserve. The shitty part about this equation is not being able to see my mom yet. It's been too many years, and now she's hours away, secluded in a high-rise apartment, staying sequestered in what I know is the lap of luxury because there is one thing about the Four Brothers: they like what they like, money isn't an object, and what they like is nice to the extreme.

"Mom said that, too, but it really sucks. Maybe in a few more days?" The hopefulness in my tone has Theo grinning. His upper lip shows a glint of his perfect teeth.

"More than likely by the weekend if things go as planned. She'll have to figure out where to go next. Charles' assets are frozen, and the house is an active crime scene since he took his work home," he explains, a matter I didn't know, so it must be a new discovery.

"Yikes. Well, she'll figure it out, or we'll help her." I go to the tips of my toes, and it's still not enough for me not to tilt my head back so far in order for us to be at eye level. Theo gets the hint. His hands move to my waist, and he lifts me off the ground. My legs immediately wrap around his waist. These days, I'm not upset one bit about him carrying me around.

"We will," he agrees.

"Have I told you lately how happy you make me?" I kiss the side of his lips, pull back, and continue, "How thankful I am to have you in my life?" Another kiss, this time on the Cupid's bow of his lip, ending with my last question, "And how much I love you?" He groans deep inside his throat and attacks my mouth with his, walking us until my body meets the railing. Our kiss isn't soft and sweet; it's hard and aggressive.

"Fuck, you make me happier than ever." He pulls back to nip at my lower lip with his teeth, soothing it with his tongue. "Best day of my life was walking into our home and finding you on your knees, when you threw your attitude back at my face when I gave you shit." He proceeds to suck my top lip into his mouth, eyes locked on one another's, neither of us not so much as blinking. "And, woman, I love you so damn much, you're permanently ingrained in my soul." He goes back to kissing me. This man, Jesus, what he does to me. He's always one-upping me with his actions, his words, his devotion to me, and I'm going to hold on to him with two hands for the rest of my life.

Epilogue

DANICA

Four Months Later

"Theo, you did not put a ring on my finger without asking. Fucking caveman," I groan out loud. I'm in bed, flat on my back, and he is doing wicked things with his tongue once again. The man is addicted to my pussy, which works for me because I'm addicted to his cock. What I was not prepared for on the day I was scheduled to walk across the stage was waking up to being engaged.

"Fairy." His voice reverberates along my slit. There is not rushing Theo. If he wants to eat me, he's going to even if we're both late. Which we will be if he doesn't stop licking me like I'm dessert for breakfast.

"Yeah, yeah, I accept." I throw out a pretend yawn. It's all an act. I pretend like I don't secretly love his caveman behavior or how he likes to carry me around. I love him and his crazy-ass antics.

"I had no doubt." His head peeks through the sheet I lifted up when I woke up at him moving my legs to accommodate his broad shoulders.

"And if I had said no?" I ask. God, this man. There are a lot of women out there who wouldn't be able to deal with him and his over-protectiveness, his obsessive behavior when he has to know my comings and goings. I do, and for good reason. Theo Goldman saved me when I was drowning, not technically, but I was drowning in misery, barely existing in this great big world. I mean, on top of having him and his friends, I now have a relationship with my mom again, who is honest to God thriving. She's working at a women's shelter, living outside of the city, and is now divorced. Mom is also no longer using her married name and went back to her maiden name, much needed if you ask me. We don't talk a lot about her time with Charles, and I'm glad. It would make me angry all over again. She talks to her friends, and, well, I talk to Theo if I'm having a moment.

"I would have made you come over and over again until all you could say is yes." His hair is a mess from sleep, and I know I'm about to have another amazing day. He won't have it any other way. "Are you ready to walk across the stage?"

"I am. Do you know what else I'm ready for?"

"What's that, fairy?" He nips at my chin. His naked body is pressed against mine, cock lying against my center.

"I threw away my birth control last night." Technically, I was supposed to throw it away last month per our agreement a while ago, but life got hectic. Theo didn't say anything when I kept taking it every morning, never missing a day. He just raised his eyebrows, looked at his watch, and then continued on.

"Fucking finally. Jesus, I thought it would take another four months. I'm going to put my baby in you, Danica. I'm going to love you and our children with everything I have." I know he will. Theo doesn't even have to say it aloud.

"I love you, and I can't wait until we have a little girl. I pray she gives you so much hell, too," I tease, knowing how Ezra is relentless with telling him little Danicas will soon invade the penthouse, and we'll be looking for a new place to live.

"We're moving. We can't raise kids in a penthouse," is his response as he pulls his hips back and bottoms out inside me, shutting me up in the best way possible.

Epilogue

THEO

Two Years Later

"DANICA, YOUR DAUGHTER SHIT HER PANTS again." Brooke, our nine-month-old daughter, is currently in the corner of our living room, red faced and grunting as she destroys yet another diaper.

"Oh no, you don't. I housed her for nine months, birthed her, had to get stitches. She has your big head, and who does she come out looking like?" We're in the kitchen of our brownstone. It took some time for us to find our house in the same neighborhood where Parker and Ezra live. We were down to the wire. Danica was ready to be in a home and nest or preparing to stay in the penthouse until Brooke was born. Luckily, our realtor found a home before it hit the market, and we looked at it that day. We offered full asking price plus an incentive, and we closed the next week.

"You. She looks just like her beautiful mother," I try to persuade her to take care of our girl and what I'm sure is going to be a complete blowout. Brooke is at the age where she's always on the go yet not crawling. The walker has been a Godsend. What hasn't been is when she hides in a corner to take a massive dump.

"No, she doesn't. Brooke looks nothing like me. Thankfully, she has my stunning personality." Danica walks around the kitchen island. A lot of things haven't changed; she still can't cook us a meal to save her life. I take on that task. What she has perfected is making homemade baby food. Which is what she's been doing all morning before we head out to meet our friends and family for dinner.

"Brooke, is Daddy really going to let you sit in a nasty diaper while Mommy slaves away at the stove all day?" My wife lays it on fucking thick. I stepped out of the living room to take a phone call, and that's when Brooke started her grunting.

"Ba-ba-ba." Brooke bangs on the tray in her walker.

"That's all you. I don't have what you have to feed her." I try to pawn the dirty job off on Danica one last time. We both know I'll be changing Brooke's diaper even if it weren't my turn.

"Theo Goldman, I'm going to kick your ass!" Danica threatens while ladling food into each container.

"Do you hear that nasty talk your mom is giving me? I get no respect around here, munchkin. Not a lick. Between you two women, I'm going to go broke and have more gray hair than your uncles." I move toward our daughter. Her little arms reach up for me. "Come on, stinky girl, we'll go change your diaper while Mom finishes up what she's doing. Then you can have her boob." Danica nurses Brooke as much as she can when she isn't working at the hospital a couple of days a week. It annoys me to no end that she won't quit and stay home full-time. Okay, it doesn't annoy me, but I'd prefer her not to work when it's not necessary. We went round and round, finally coming to an agreement that she'd work part-time, for now. Once another little one is in the picture, she'd re-evaluate, but I've heard her grumble lately that she's tired the day after work. I keep biding my time and biting my tongue. She'll quit when she's ready. Especially when Brooke has another sleep regression, which is coming, if last night is anything to go by.

"I've got her." I pick Brooke up. She's all smiles for a little girl who's had a massive blowout. It's up her back and coming out of her diaper and clothing. "We're heading to the bathroom. Feel free to help me. What did you feed her?" I ask my wife, holding Brooke out in front of me in case of any leakage.

"She's teething." As if that explains everything to me. I walk down the hall, using my elbow to turn on the light in the bathroom. I look at Brooke's back in the mirror, and yep, it's going to be a messy one. I go through the process of starting the bath while putting her in the ring we have suctioned to the bathtub. As soon as the water is on and at a warm temperature, I'll go through the process of stripping her down.

"You got it handled in here, or do you need a hand?" I look over my shoulder. My wife is fucking gorgeous, still small in size with some newly found curves.

"Yeah. You want to grab a change of clothes or undress her?" I'd have handled it either way, but I'm not an idiot and will take all the help I can get when it comes to having Danica by my side.

"You go grab the clothes. I'll work on getting her ready for her bath." She moves to my side and goes to her knees. "Oh, girlfriend, you're cute, but man, you're a mess. Those teeth are not being fair to you." Brooke smiles up at her with a gummy grin.

"When do you think she'll finally break a tooth and not have blowouts because of them?"

"I'm not sure. Millie told me the same thing happened to their little one and to be prepared." She shrugs her shoulders.

"Well, shit, literally. I'll be right back." I go to stand up, but Danica's hand goes to my forearm.

"I hope you're prepared to do this with two in the next eight months or so." There are tears in her eyes. My throat bobs with emotion I'm not putting a name to.

"Fuck, yeah, I am. God, I love you guys. All of you." My hand touches her abdomen.

"I love you, Theo, forever," she replies the same moment Brooke throws a toy at me, getting me sopping wet. "I'd say she has her mom's aim, too." Our plans to head out the door to meet our friends are forgotten. We hang out with Brooke while she plays in the bath after we wash her and talk about what our life is going to be like with two children under two next year.

I hope you enjoyed Theo and Danica's story and will consider leaving a review. While this may be the end of the Billionaire Playboys and boy is it always sad to see them go. They are chirping in my ear and saying we want one more

**bonus scene. Click the link below if
you'd like to read!**

<insert link>

**The next book in the Men in Charge
Series is coming August 27th, each book
in this series can be read as a
standalone. So if you like a forbidden
small town romance, Baring it All may be
right up your alley and releases August
27th!**

Amazon

Prologue
Two Weeks Earlier

Stormy

"Harder, yes, right there," I stop in my tracks,
knowing that voice, figuring my best friend is
hooking up with one of the groomsmen. Which
sucks because I need her, this God awful dress I
somehow was roped into wearing at this God
awful ceremony, not to mention the God awful
amount of people. Attention good or bad is not
my idea of fun, three hundred people, mostly
Zach's family, conglomerates, and half the

fucking town, yeah, no thanks. Except I got railroaded by Zach's mom, a force to be reckoned with, wearing me so far down it was easier than standing my ground.

"Fuck yeah, you like being my dirty little secret, don't you, Mel," ice runs through my veins, I fucking know that voice. The voice behind the heavy wooden door, inside this monstrosity of a ceremony location, a freaking clubhouse. I wanted a small intimate wedding, friends and family, one hundred people max. My hand goes to my chest, making sure my heart is still beating, lucky for me it is, unlucky for me it is too. There's no way I'm imagining Zach's voice, I'd know it anywhere on any day of the week. My hand wraps around the silver knob, slowly turning the handle, trying to stay as quiet as possible, as if this is a horrible dream and once I open the door I'll wake up. Except I know the possibility is moot, this is what horror movies are made of, like the leading character running upstairs when the killer is in the house instead of leaving the house. Well, look at me, staying rooted in place, opening a door to the scene in front of me, my best friend or ex-best friend is currently bent at the waist, maid of honor dress hiked up while my fiancée pistons his hips in and out of her body, and son of a biscuit eater I'd bet my last dollar no condom is being used either. Which means my wedding day, a day meant to be happy, I'm not expecting it to be

Cinderella magnificent but this, this is the last thing I expected.

I could scream, I could cry, I could do both at once, instead I take a deep breath, open the door wider, allowing any passersby to get a birds eye view of the free porn show, and I top it off even better, I clap. A standing ovation of one, it takes them a moment, each of them stuttering in their sexual escapades, "Bravo," I finally say, my hands come together in a rhythmic applaud, repeating it until Melanie and Zach get the idea they're no longer alone.

"It's not what it looks like," Zach pulls out of Melanie, sloppily, just as I figured. I'll be adding a doctor's appointment a long with an STD testing, yay fucking me.

"Are you fucking kidding me," I'm calm, cool, and collective, my namesake doing nothing for me right now because I should be angry and crying, yet none of those hit me. I'm left feeling upset at myself more than anything, did my friendship with Melissa mean so little to me that she'd toss away more than twenty years of friendship for sex with Zach, Zach who I thought was going to be my end all be all. Boy was I wrong, assuming really does make an ass out of you and me.

"Stormy, please let us explain," Mel tries to cajole me, as if I'm one of her students at the elementary school. I watch as she fixes her dress so at least I'm no longer seeing her naked ass or Zach's either. My eyes close, breathing deeply, attempting to figure out what to do next, how I'm going to stand in front of three hundred people, tell them the show is over and they missed it the grooms dressing room.

"I don't think there's much to explain, between Zach's it's not what I think. What did his dick fall into your vag or should we talk about how your so in love with a cheating dirt bag, you'd willingly ruin everything to get what you want," both of them are stunned silent, Zach looking everywhere but at me, the horrid dress his mother insisted I wear, the venue she chose, down to the flowers in the reception area. This was never the wedding I envisioned and Zach was never the man I was going to live with till the end of time.

"It's not like that, you have to believe me," Mel attempts to step towards me, my hand flies up, holding her back because there's no telling what I'll do if I have to smell the two of them on her body. It's one thing for the room to permeate the scent of sex, it's another to have it flaunted under your nose, which I mean. Isn't that what they've been doing all along? Zach remains silent, thankfully his tuxedo pants are zipped up and I no longer have to see the evidence of their relationship.

"How long have you two been screwing each other behind my back?" I ask, morbid curiosity creeps up. I'd like to say maybe I was part of the issue but I know with every depth of my being it's not a me thing, it's a them thing. I witnessed this whole scenario play out with my parents in my teen years, a fourteen year old girl watching their dad walk out on them to start a new family with a new wife, it hits you bone deep. Not once did my mom make me feel anything else than loved, picking up the broken pieces of what she didn't leave behind while brushing herself off, waiting to cry at night when I was supposed to be asleep. The next morning, she'd wake up and do it all over again until one night I didn't hear her cry, I heard her laugh at a television show, and that was when I realized my mom is stronger than any woman I've ever met.

"Stormy, what difference does it make?" My eyes narrow at Zach, his hands are in his pockets, tie askew, hair a mess. The man in front of me isn't the man I thought I knew, my best friend, even worse, betrayal, Zach and Melissa have done the worst of the worst.

"Six months," Melissa clears her throat, forging on with the conversation, "We're in love, Stormy." I watch as my now former best friend moves closer to my now former fiancée, the two of them locking hands together, and that's all I can take, needing bleach for my eyes in a permanent kind of way, someone needs to tell the guests what's going on and I need three bottles of champagne stat. I don't bother responding, my give a damn is busted, those two lying, cheating scumbags deserve one another. While I was dealing with his nutcase of a mother wanting a perfect wedding, catering to her every whim while Zach was supposedly working well into the night and couldn't so much as help when I asked him to wade between his mother and I. It's why I'm in this stupid dress, at this stupid country club, with a stupid amount of people I didn't want in the first place, obviously Zach didn't either. He could have been a man about it, talked to me, I'd have at least been a bit understanding as it stands I'm going to have to tell my mother, aunt, Zach's mother, ugh maybe I won't actually touch the subject with her. I know how that song and dance will go, she'll blame the entirety on me .

"Good luck, he told me that too. I'm leaving, figure out this shit on your own," I leave the room, there are no tears streaming down my face, that should be telling, right? I should at least be feeling a gamut of emotions, except I'm not, I'm just done.

"It's different," an obnoxious cackle comes from the back of my throat, head rolling back on my neck. Apparently everything is hitting me all at once, the wedding, dealing with Zach's awful mother, my own mother trying to smooth things over while still keeping the peace, absolutely hating how I've rolled over and taken the verbal abuse, and now this, now freaking this. My chest tightens, fingers tingling, fuck even more toes that are scrunched into a pair of too high heels are, my hands go to my décolletage, nails scratching at the lace feeling like I'm unable to drag enough air into my lungs. If this is what dying is like then please let there be white sandy beaches, the ocean air, the scent of my favorite coconut, pineapple, and sugar lotion on the other side. Those are my last thoughts as stars appear beneath my closed eyelids, unsure who closed them because I assure you I did not decide to feel like I'm this helpless person in front of Zach and Melissa, no way, no how, never ever, yet that's exactly what happens. My whole body shuts down and that's all she wrote.

———

Griffin

Worthless piece of shit, I was walking down the hall looking for the john when I stumbled upon my niece and what everyone knows is the groom looking disheveled, one plus one equals mother fucking two. On any given day I'd keep to myself and walk the hell away, I've got enough drama in my life the way it is, running the local bar, dealing with waitresses, bar backs, alcohol distributers, and that doesn't include the damn customers getting drunk off their ass, acting like damn idiots. Today wasn't that day, hell this whole Saturday affair isn't a place you'd find me willingly and if it wasn't for this damn small town, I wouldn't be here but for appearances sakes, it's where I am and at a damn good time.

"Jesus, you two the reason for this?" Stormy, the bride is currently in my arms, head lolled back, one arm bracketed beneath the back of her knees the other beneath her neck, "Got nothing to say for yourselves," I quirk an eyebrow, Mel has the good sense to look away, Zach is too busy opening and closing his mouth, like a bass fish after it's been caught from the lake, "Figures," I grumble, my eyes move from the pair of dumb asses.

I don't bother having a one-sided conversation, the way Stormy is, I'm willing to bet the two people in this room are the reason she's in the position she is now. It doesn't matter that I'm walking away, carrying the bride of this charade, leaving the groom passed out from fainting, she was lucky I double stepped in. Luckily, no one is around when I walk out of the room, the hallway is empty, and I'm trying to find a room the isn't permeated with sex, hoping Stormy doesn't come awake in my arms, do an about face, and hit me in the face.

"Fuck," I grumble, my hand beneath her knees tries the doorknob, finding it locked, so we go to the next. This place has more rooms than a luxury hotel, the second knob twists open, and I'm stepping inside, kicking the door shut with my foot, locking it will have to wait, "Stormy, can you hear me?" I ask as I set her down on the couch.

"Ugh," she grumbles, eyes opening, a dazed look on her face when she notices it's me.

"You good?" Stormy rolls over, I'm unsure of how to take that until she pulls it together enough to say, "Help, off. I need to breathe," her long dainty fingers are trying to pull on the buttons.

"Son of a bitch," I figure my hand knocks hers out of the way, working at them as fast as I can and still it's not fast enough for my liking, "Hold still, Stormy, don't move a fucking inch," my pocket knife, flicking the blade open, my eyes meet hers, as she's looking over her shoulder, I'm willing to bet this contraption of a damn dress is the culprit for her collapsing all along.

"Hurry," with a steady hand I slice through the fabric, the slicing of fabric echoes throughout what can be considered a gentleman's lounge. I was about to pull my cell phone out of my pocket to call an ambulance, when Stormy came to, talking about her lack of breath which is why when the last button on her dress gives ways, she's taking a series of deep breaths. The damn thing was buttoned clear from her neck down to her lower back.

"Feel better?" I ask, trying not to notice the expanse of skin she's showing off. I close my knife, placing it back in my pocket, "Whoa, whoa, whoa, you think getting up that fast is smart?" my hands come out, unsure of what to do in order to hold her back from doing more bad than good.

"I'm fine, I need to get out of here. Me and a bottle Jose Cuervo have a date, maybe two bottles," Stormy isn't listening to reason. Instead I help her up, making sure she's steady on her feet before letting her go.

"Come on, I'll get you out of here. Plus, the saying goes, the best way to get over someone is to get under someone else," Stormy takes my out stretched hand, allowing me to lead the way, a ripped dress, hand holding the front of her dress in order for it not to fall down and give me a view I have no right wanting, her hair is a mess, dark hair tumbling from the once what I'm sure was an upswept style. All I know is if anyone is going to make her forget today it'll be me and my thick dick.

Amazon

About the Author

Tory Baker is a mom and dog mom, living on the coast of sunny Florida where she enjoys the sun, sand, and water anytime she can. Most of the time you can find her outside with her laptop, soaking up the rays while writing about Alpha men, sassy heroines, and always with a guaranteed happily ever after.

Sign up to receive her **Newsletter** for all the latest news!

Tory Baker's Readers is where you see and hear all of the news first!

Acknowledgments

This is about to get very long and very wordy because that's just who I am. I've got so many people to thank and shout out that I hope no one is forgotten. When I set out about change this year, I was all freaking in. I'm extremely fortunate you all are taking this wild ride with me. The depth in these stories it fills my heart up with a joy I lost along the way and my cup couldn't runneth over without your support!

To my kids: A & A without you I'd be a shell of myself. You helped me find myself in a moment of darkness. Thank you for picking up the slack around the house while I was knee deep in this deadline, cooking, cleaning, and taking care of Remi (our big lug of a Weimaraner). I love you to infinity times infinity.

Jordan: Oh my lanta, the hand holding, the me calling you hysterically crying or laughing, day or night, good or bad. I love you bigger than outer space. If it weren't for you pushing me to write, to see the potential in me, I wouldn't be here.

Mayra: My sprinting partner extraordinaire. Girlfriend, we made it through 2022 ahead of schedule. One day I will fly my butt to California to hug you!

Julia: How do you deal with me and my extra sprinkling of commas? The real MVP, the one who deals with my scatterbrained self, missing deadlines, rescheduling like crazy, and the person I live vicariously through social media.

Amie Vermaas Jones: Thank you for always and I do mean always helping me on my last minute shit. It never fails that I'm sending you an SOS asking for your eyes. Beach days are happening and SOON!

Nashara McClaeb: The friend I owe margs and wings with a hockey game. Thank you for always being a message away!

Thank you for being here, reading, not just my books but any Author's stories. We do appreciate you more than you know, the reason why we can live out our dream is for readers, bloggers, bookstagrammers, bookmakers, Authors, and everyone in between. THANK YOU!

All this to say, I am and will always be forever grateful, love you all!

Also by Tory Baker

Men in Charge

Make Her Mine

Staking His Claim

Secret Obsession

Baring it All

Billionaire Playboys

Playing Dirty

Playing with Fire

Playing With Her

Playing His Games

Playing to Win

Vegas After Dark Series

All Night Long

Late Night Caller

One More Night

About Last Night

One Night Stand

Hart of Stone Family

Tease Me

Hold Me

Kiss Me

Please Me

Touch Me

Feel Me

Diamondback MC Second Gen.

Obsessive

Seductive

Addictive

Protective

Deceptive

Diamondback MC

Dirty

Wild

Bare

Wet

Filthy

Sinful

Wicked

Thick

Bad Boys of Texas

Harder

Bigger

Deeper

Hotter

Faster

Hot Shot Series

Fox

Cruz

Jax

Saint

Getting Dirty Series

Serviced (Book 1)

Primed (Book 2)

Licked (Book 3)

Hammered (Book 4)

Nighthawk Security

Never Letting Go (Easton and Cam's story)

Claiming Her (Book 1)

Craving More (Book 2)

Sticky Situations (Travis and Raelynn's story)

Needing Him (Book 3)

Only His (Book 4)

Carter Brothers Series

Just One Kiss

Just One Touch

Just One Promise

Finding Love Series

A Love Like Ours

A Love To Cherish

A Love That Lasts

Stand Alone Titles

Nailed

Going All In

What He Wants

Accidental Daddy

Love Me Forever

Gettin' Lucky

It's Her Love

Meant To Be

Breaking His Rules

Can't Walk Away

Carried Away

Unwrapping His Present

Tempting the Judge

Made in United States
Orlando, FL
18 June 2025